# HUMMINGBIRD

## FRAN GRANT

FRAN GRANT
PRESS

ISBN: 978-1-9163162-3-2

Written by Fran Grant

Cover illustration by Alana McCarthy

Formatted by Author Services by Sarah

## Prologue

I can't remember exactly when he stopped being the perfect stepdad, or even if he ever was one. Perhaps that was just other people's perception of him. I can remember, though, the first time he hit me. And the first time he crept into my room at night.

## Kya

It's a sad fact, but it's true – some people genuinely believe that a seemingly sincere apology, coupled with a promise not to repeat their harmful behaviour, is enough for everyone to forget the whole thing and act like nothing's happened. *Let's put it behind us and move on*, is a phrase I've grown used to hearing, or *He didn't mean it. You're like a daughter to him.* I'm not, and we both know it. Lizzie is his daughter. In his eyes, I'm just the baggage from Mum's first marriage.

I was eleven, and Mum was heavily pregnant with Lizzie. Like most eleven year olds, I didn't want to eat my cabbage, so I moaned and fussed while Mum tried to cajole me. I wasn't being awkward – it genuinely made me gag, still does to this day. I can smell it now, all warm and buttery and sweaty. Then out of the blue he, and by *he* I mean my mum's husband, leapt up off his chair, his plate flying off the table in the process, sending cabbage and gravy splattering everywhere. He lunged towards me, eyes bulging out of their sockets, frothing at the mouth. He looked so hideous, so monstrous, that for a fraction of a second I thought he was messing around. But he wasn't. He grabbed a fistful of cabbage, wet and buttery, and tried to force it into my mouth. I was shocked and frightened and despite the natural urge to shout out, I had to fight hard to keep my mouth locked shut against the onslaught of slimy cabbage. Scared and angry, I writhed, trying to get away, tears streaming down my cheeks, but he had a tight grip on the collar of my school shirt with his other hand, and the more I struggled the tighter his grip became. I could hear Mum shouting at him to get off me, but she just stood there, stock still, with her hands protectively holding her enormous pregnant belly. I remember hearing words like *ungrateful little bitch* and *not wasting money in this house,* and as he shouted angry spittle flew from his mouth and spattered my face, filling me with revulsion. I don't know how long it lasted, it could have been ten seconds or it could have been minutes, but eventually he let go of my shirt and gave up trying to cram the cabbage into my mouth. He flew out of the room, swiping more plates off the table as he passed, and slammed the back door behind him. I fell to the floor, stunned, butter smeared all over my face, feeling humiliated, angry, helpless. My lips felt bruised and swollen on the outside, sore and bleeding on the inside where they'd been pressed so hard against my teeth. Mum sent me to my room while she cleared up the broken plates and wiped food debris off the carpets and walls. I sat on my bed and hugged my knees to my chest. The shock of what had just happened had stunned me into silence.

I switched the TV on as a distraction, desperately seeking some normality, and watched a documentary on hummingbirds. I sat, numb, staring blankly at the screen, not really listening, just watching, staring, marvelling at the hummingbirds, at all their pretty colours. I tried to push thoughts such as *If he can do it once, he'll do it again* out of my head, and instead focused on the narrator's calming voice telling me that hummingbirds' hearts beat over twelve hundred times a minute. I've never forgotten this fact.

I heard him come back some time later and I listened with trepidation at my bedroom door, ready for Mum to shout, hit him with *How dare you treat my daughter like that?* and tell him she was leaving him. But it never came. I heard him snivel and weep and when I looked through the bannister, I saw Mum comforting him. *She* was comforting *him*. She came to my room and said he was sorry and that he would never do it again. I felt doubly betrayed, and looking back, that was the moment I felt like I was losing my mum.

That night I dreamt of the hummingbird from the TV. It was trapped in a bell jar that sat in the middle of a round table, and it was frantically trying to get out, tapping on the glass with its long, narrow beak. I sensed its fear and I felt incredibly sorrowful, but I was powerless to help as I was just an invisible presence, hovering in the air, looking down on the bell jar. I moved closer and I marvelled at the tiny bird's beauty, its iridescent colours blending from blue to green to purple. It stopped tapping on the glass and turned its colourful head to face me, a look of desperation in its tiny black eyes that seemed to say *Help me!* Then, right before my eyes, it disintegrated into a pile of powdery dust, and just like that, it was no more.

## Kya

To seek protection from a parent only to be met with disbelief, denial, or even blame, is damaging and hurtful beyond words. It cuts deep, and the wound never fully heals. I soon learned that Mum would simply dismiss, disregard or outright negate my attempts to speak up about what was going on.

'But why can't you just leave him?' I begged, after that first incident with the cabbage. 'You've been together less than a year!'

'He's a good man, Kya, it was just a one off. He's never had a daughter before, he's just getting used to things.'

'I'm not his daughter!'

'And I'm not bringing up another baby alone! You don't know how hard the last eleven years have been, trying to make ends meet, struggling as a single mother.'

'We were fine as we were, it was perfect when it was just me and you!'

'We could barely afford our rent, Kya. Have you forgotten I had to work two jobs?'

It was true. She worked part time in a care home while I

was at school, and then she took on cleaning jobs for neighbours, running their errands, fetching their shopping, just to get some extra cash. But I was happy when it was just us. We didn't have much money, I knew that, because I couldn't go on school trips or get fancy pencil cases or fashionable rucksacks like all the other kids, but we were happy. We didn't often have treats, but when we did, they would form some of my favourite memories – sharing a bag of vinegary chips, renting a movie from the corner shop, or making perfume using flowers we'd picked at the park. Those times were magical. Our cupboards were usually pretty bare, but somehow we always had a meal. Mum would sometimes bring food back from the care home, leftover vegetable curry or pasta bake. Sometimes we'd eat beans on toast for three days in a row, but they were the best beans on toast. Occasionally, Mum would bring some ingredients home from work and we'd bake buttery biscuits together, then curl up and eat them with a mug of warm milk and a story. We couldn't afford to go to the fair when it came to town, so instead we made sticky sandwiches with the honey the old man across the road had given Mum for helping him with his shopping, and we got under a blanket and watched our favourite movie. She would walk me to school and I always felt so safe with her. I was her whole world and she was mine. We were always laughing, talking, singing, hugging, holding hands. Mother and daughter. Best friends. Safe as houses.

'He looks after us. He's a good man really. And when the baby comes along, we'll be one big happy family. Things will settle down, I promise.'

That was five years ago. Things did calm down for a while. Lizzie came along, and she was the apple of his eye, but he would look at me with contempt. Then Mum got a job at the new care home working night shifts, and things got worse.

## Lizzie

K ya is the best big sister ever. She's sixteen and I am only five so she is my *really big* sister. When Mummy goes to work at night, Kya does my bath time and then she snuggles up with me and reads my bedtime story. I make her read my favourite story about the bear who can't sleep, because she always does the voices right. She's funny. Then in the morning she makes my toast just how I like it – she cuts it into little triangles and picks the lumps out of the jam. When I grow up I want to be just like her.

## Kya

A ll children should have the right to feel safe in their own homes, but if they don't, it changes their life view completely. Their belief that the world is a safe place and that all grown-ups are good and trustworthy is shattered. The bullying was subtle at first, creeping up slowly. It was wrapped up as harmless teasing, but I knew he got a thrill out of humiliating me in front of my friends. He'd pick a fight, try to expose my embarrassing secrets, or make fun of my shortcomings in front of them, and if I tried to object he'd blow up and fly off into one of his rages. Then came the name calling, the constant criticism, the sarcasm with a spiteful undertone. The angry jibes, the blaming, the scapegoating. Constantly belittling me. It wasn't long before it escalated to red-faced yelling and angry reminders of *whose house this is!* And then there was the time he punched me in the stomach for daring to stand up for myself. In the early days, he would come up to my room afterwards and sit on my bed, crying and snivelling. Then he'd try to hug me and tell me it was difficult for him. He would look at me in a way I could never describe as a child, I just knew it made my flesh crawl. Now that I'm older, he never apologises. I never see remorse, just anger and contempt, and he still makes my skin creep. It's a horrible feeling lying in bed at night and not feeling safe, listening out for every noise. But they won't let me put a lock on my bedroom door. *What if there's a fire?* they say. Most kids fear noises outside the house. I fear noises inside the house, like footsteps walking up the stairs, and the creak of the floorboard outside my bedroom door.

Last year a girl from my school got cancer and everyone rallied around her. I'm not saying she didn't deserve the sympathy and support, but her suffering was heroic, whereas my suffering has always felt like a source of humiliation and isolation. You can see cancer. Or a broken leg. You can't see this. You can't see the suffering caused by living with someone who goes out of their way to torment you, especially in front of your friends, seemingly enjoying the distress it causes you. You're powerless to defend yourself, so the anger builds, but it has nowhere to go so it festers, poisoning your insides, changing your cells at a molecular level. So I stopped having friends round, because the fear of him creating a scene caused me too much angst. They thought it was strange at first, thought I was weird and antisocial, but eventually they stopped trying, and I was relieved, happy to sit in the library alone and concentrate on my studies. I learnt to shut off my emotions, hardened myself to everyone and everything around me. Grappling with the aftermath of an argument or one of his outbursts takes tremendous energy, and often all I have left is just enough to stay in coping mode. I don't have the strength to undergo any further trauma, it takes everything I have just to carry on. Living in survival mode is exhausting, constantly reminding myself that I just have to get through this last stretch of high school plus two years of college, then I can escape to university.

There have been one or two occasions, after particularly

hideous fights with him, where I've thought death seemed more inviting than life. As Shakespeare said, *'Why not death, rather than living torment?'* I often wonder why people fear death, more than they fear pain, suffering or humiliation. Life can be far more painful and torturous than death. Once you welcome death, the pain ends. It sometimes feels like it could be a welcome break.

But for now, I'll find solace in my books. Eventually, they will save me.

## Lizzie

**D**addy is the best daddy ever! I came home from school today and he gave me a big box, and when I opened it I found the shiny red shoes with the silver buckle, the ones I wanted from the TV! I put them on and did a twirl and everyone laughed and Daddy hugged me and told me I was the best daughter in the world and that I deserved them. I wanted to wear them to bed but Mummy laughed and said I couldn't wear them to bed, but I could keep them on my rug. I'm so excited, I can't wait to wear them to school tomorrow. I lay in bed looking at my shoes on the rug and I heard Mummy and Daddy using their loud voices downstairs. Daddy's was loudest. He said he doesn't care if Kya needs new shoes too, she can't have any as she doesn't deserve them. Mummy said he was being not fair, and he said it's his money and that's that. Sometimes he is a bit mean to Kya. I asked him why once, and he said it's because she is a lousy teenager. He said I am his princess though and that he would never shout at me. I don't think Kya is bad, she plays with me and reads me stories all the time. She cuddles me in bed and strokes my hair. She calls me goldilocks. My hair is not like hers. Hers is black. And she doesn't have blue eyes like me, hers are green, like my bright green marbles. She smells of those sticks she burns in her room. Tonight she is reading me my favourite story about the baby bear who can't sleep because there is too much dark in the cave. Kya says I am her baby bear and she will always protect me. I don't need protecting from the dark though, I have a night light shaped like a mushroom.

# Kya

The childminder has just been to collect Lizzie. She picks her up at 8:15am on the mornings that Mum's on an overnight shift, and takes her to school. Lizzie is so confident for a five year old, always happy and smiling. I watch her through the window, bursting with excitement as she runs towards the childminder's car.

'Look what Daddy bought me! They're the ones from the TV that I've always wanted!' she squeals as she twirls round on the pavement, showing off her shiny red shoes.

'Well aren't you a lucky girl, hey?' The childminder beams as she bends down to admire Lizzie's shoes.

'I've got the best daddy in the world!'

'You most certainly have, Dear,' she smiles. 'You are both very lucky girls indeed.' She looks around for me and I duck behind the curtain. I know what she's thinking – perfect house, perfect family, doting father with the all-important job. He's standing on the driveway in his crisp white shirt, smiling and laughing, picking Lizzie up and swinging her around while she giggles uncontrollably, kissing her on the cheek. It's all for show. I feel like screaming, *I'm not lucky! This is all an act!*

*Don't fall for it – he's a monster underneath!* But he has everyone fooled.

✧

I dread these mornings. Now they're gone I can literally feel the air change inside the house. His fake smile has disappeared and his fake cheery voice has returned to one infused with venom. I'm running late for school and I want to get out of the house as quickly as possible. I grab my bag and make for the door.

'Sit down, you haven't eaten breakfast.'

'I don't want any, I'm not hungry.' I never feel hungry in the morning. My stomach is always churning, knotted. 'I've got a banana in my bag.'

'You are not leaving this house until you've had breakfast.'

'But I...'

'SIT!' he screams.

He points at a bowl of thick, lumpy porridge opposite him. I sit down and try to eat it, even though I don't like porridge, and it's a huge bowl. All because *he* likes it and thinks everyone else should live by his rules. My stomach is knotted. He's sitting there slurping his porridge and it's dribbling down his chin. I stare at him with loathing and the anger rises up inside me, clawing at my insides, burning my throat.

'I'm done.' I get up to leave the table.

'SIT down. You will eat every last bit!'

I swear he enjoys these mornings when Mum's not here, gets off on it in some sick way. He loves any opportunity to try and control me, bully me, break me. The anger boils inside me and I feel the hatred creeping through my veins. I want to scream at him, tell him I hate him, tell him he can't control me. The humiliation of not being able to stick up for myself, and the fear and frustration eats away at my soul and makes me even more irascible.

'No!' I shout, my voice wobbly. 'I don't have to eat it. You can't force me to eat breakfast!'

In a split second he's on his feet, the contents of his bowl all over the table, and he's heading towards me, his body gorilla-like, his face puce, his eyes glaring like a madman's. Thoughts of him force feeding me porridge race through my mind as he grabs me by my jacket collar. His contorted face is right next to mine and I try to turn away. His eyes glare with rage as he shouts something about *learning to do as I'm told* and *It's about time I respected him!* His breath is pungent, and spittle mixed with porridge is flying out of his mouth and landing on my face. Eventually he lets go of my collar and I push past him, grab my bag and run for the door. I run up the street and don't stop till I've rounded the corner at the end and ducked into the graveyard. I want to scream and shout as the violent and uncontrollable rage rises within me, and although I try and suppress it, it comes out as angry tears, furiously burning my face as I slump down against the wall. I hear a twig crack and I think I see a boy with black hair duck behind a tree. I'm too exhausted to care. I don't want to live, if I have to live this life. I would rather die. Or maybe I'd rather he died. It would be so easy to drive a knife into him and kill him. The thing I'm finding more and more difficult is to stay strong inside, bide my time, and make it impossible for him to cut me down. And I ask myself, if the desire to kill and the opportunity to kill coincided – would I be able to stop myself?

## Lizzie

We had my favourite dinner tonight, spaghetti bolognese with cheese on top, but Kya wasn't home. She stays late at school sometimes to study. Mummy and Daddy were using their loud voices and talking about Kya being a bad girl this morning. Daddy said Kya acts up whenever Mummy is out of the house and that she is getting uncontrollable. Mummy said he should try and keep out of her way and he said he tries to but she provokes him.

Now Daddy has gone out, and Kya is back. I'm supposed to be brushing my teeth upstairs but I'm sitting on the landing with Bunny, listening. Mummy and Kya are using their loud voices now. My teacher always says you should use your indoor voice when you're inside. Kya is crying and keeps shouting *He's a bully!* Who is a bully? Is she being bullied at school? Mummy is saying *Why do you always have to put me in the middle?* Kya starts up the stairs so I run into the bathroom. She slams her bedroom door and turns her music up really loud. She wouldn't do that if Daddy was home, he would get really cross. I go to her room and open the door, it smells of the sticks she's burning.

'Kya, are you reading my story tonight?'

'Come here, baby girl,' she says to me.

I climb onto her bed and crawl into her arms. She's been crying.

'Why are you crying, Kya?'

'It's ok, baby girl, you don't have to worry,' she strokes my hair, 'I'll make sure you never have to go through this.'

'Go through what, Kya?' Maybe she's talking about the bully again.

But she doesn't answer me. She just pulls me in tighter and kisses the top of my head like she always does.

## Kya

I dream of the hummingbird again tonight. The exact same one, with hues of teal green, blue and purple. Someone is squeezing the life out of it, literally. All I can see are big fat fingers clasped tightly around the tiny bird as it squawks with fear, it's eyes pleading. The fingers grip tighter still, and the long, narrow beak of the bird desperately opens and closes but there's no longer any sound coming out. I am powerless to help, as the fist squeezes, squeezes, squeezes until *pop!* Its tiny black eyes pop clean out of its head and its body goes limp. I wake up sweating, my own chest feeling constricted as if it's me who is being squeezed.

# Zak

There she is, the girl from the graveyard. I've not stopped thinking about her since I first saw her there last week. I've never seen anyone crying at the same time as looking so furious. Someone must have really upset her. I wanted to go and check up on her but I would've looked like a crazy stalker coming out from behind that tree. I've seen her walk that way to school every day since then, from a distance, and now I see her in the library too. She always sits in the same corner seat, her body language warning people not to approach her. I don't think I've ever noticed anyone the way I'm noticing her. Her black hair, her pale skin, those bright green eyes – how would I even describe that colour? Emerald. She wears the same uniform as everyone else at the high school but she wears it in her own way, almost rebellious, long sleeved black top under her white school shirt, black tights, chunky black Doc Martens. I can't decide what I'm drawn to most about her. Her moody look suggests she'd bite someone's head off if they approached her. She doesn't want attention. Her body language shows she doesn't want company. She's sultry, elusive, and God, she's sexy. Those red lips, and the way her glossy black hair rests perfectly on her shoulders and flicks out. And then my heart nearly jumps out of my chest as I notice she's reading a book about Jim Morrison, *The Lords and the New Creatures: The Original Published Poetry of Jim Morrison*. In all my seventeen years I've never known anyone else who's into Jim Morrison. I don't know for sure that she adores him like I do, but she's reading his poetry, and that's a good sign. An incredible sign! I need to know her. I yearn to know her. I'm feeling something I've never felt before just from looking at someone. But I can't approach her, so I decide I'll look her up on the school messenger system.

## Kya

I saw him again today. The boy in black. I was sitting in the library and he was standing over by the stairs, staring at me. I'm sure he was. I ignored him, obviously. I think he must live near me as I've seen him taking the shortcut through the graveyard too. There's something about him that I can't quite put my finger on. He's definitely not my type, not that I have a type. Not that I'm even interested in guys right now, I just want to focus on getting my grades, getting through college and getting into a university far, far away from here. He looks different from all the other guys. I can't tell what colour eyes he's got, his longish black hair keeps flopping over his face, but I can feel them burning into me as he stares. He doesn't wear uniform so he must be in the sixth form, and he's always, always dressed head to toe in black. Perhaps he's a vampire.

## Zak

It's taken me hours of scrolling through profile pictures of everyone on the school messenger system. Past all the typical profile pics of pouty girls with their flawless hair and makeup, and I wonder how many selfies didn't make the cut. My black raven (as I've been thinking of her, seeing as I don't know her name) couldn't be more different from all those validation seekers, who so desperately want to be noticed. And suddenly I see her, profile name Angry_Teenager. I'd recognise her anywhere. She's not quite glaring at the camera, but she's not smiling either. Her emerald eyes have whole worlds inside them and I want to reach through the screen and touch her pale cheek, to see if it really is as soft as it looks. And those red lips. Ok, get yourself together, Zak. I need to change my profile picture first, use one that's less dorky and more bad boy. I can't imagine she likes good boys. I need to change my name to something more alluring too, like hers. Tall_Dark_Handsome. No, too corny, she'll hate that. Tall_Dark_Dangerous. Perfect.

## Kya

Mum's not working tonight, so the house is fairly relaxed. Well, as relaxed as it can be. It feels like I've been tightly coiled for so long I've forgotten what happy and relaxed is actually like. I'm doing my homework online, TV on quietly in the background to break up the silence, and something beeps. The school messenger app – odd, I never use that, I hate social media of any kind. I have a message.

*Tall_Dark_Dangerous:*
Hello, I love you, won't you tell me your name?

It's him. The boy in black. His profile picture is a bit blurred, but it's definitely him. I type my reply without hesitating.

*Angry_Teenager:*
Okaaay... Jim Morrison fan or weirdo stalker?

*Tall_Dark_Dangerous:*
Definitely the former. And I saw you in the library today

reading *The Lords and the New Creatures*. I have a copy at home. Also, you live near me. I see you walking through the graveyard.

*Angry_Teenager:*
So you are a stalker?

*Tall_Dark_Dangerous:*
Would you like me more if I was?

*Angry_Teenager:*
Er…

*Tall_Dark_Dangerous:*
Don't worry, I'm not a stalker. Just a massive fan of The Doors and Jim Morrison, and I've never met anyone else who likes him. So, will you tell me your name?

*Angry_Teenager:*
How about you tell me how you found me on here? I don't use my name on this for a reason. Prefer to stay anonymous.

*Tall_Dark_Dangerous:*
Well, you are elusive. It took me hours of scrolling through profile pics until I found yours. But I'd recognise you anywhere.

*Angry_Teenager:*
Stalker.

*Tall_Dark_Dangerous:*
You are captivating. But you look like you'd rip my head off if I approached you in person.

*Angry_Teenager:*
Is that a compliment?

*Tall_Dark_Dangerous:*
I should have said beautifully captivating.

*Angry_Teenager:*
Kya.

*Tall_Dark_Dangerous:*
Is that code for something?

*Angry_Teenager:*
My name is Kya. It means diamond in the sky, apparently.

*Tall_Dark_Dangerous:*
Well nice to meet you, Kya. I'm Zak, a boy with a perfect heart and a wonderful soul. His ability to make you smile is unbelievable. Sarcasm is his primary language.

*Angry_Teenager:*
I like the sarcasm bit. Not sure about the smiling.

*Tall_Dark_Dangerous:*
You don't like to smile? I bet I could make you smile.

*Angry_Teenager:*
Probably not.

*Tall_Dark_Dangerous:*
Oh yes, angry teenager. I forgot. So how'd you get into The Doors?

*Angry_Teenager:*

I like his poetry, it's abstract. He was always prophesying about death, right? Borderline psychotic. I like that. I'm also intrigued as to why people adored him if he was so reckless, selfish and mercurial. Abusive even. You?

*Tall_Dark_Dangerous:*
His music. My dad idolised him. He was a massive fan.

*Angry_Teenager:*
Was?

*Tall_Dark_Dangerous:*
He died. A while back. He left me all his Doors records and memorabilia.

*Angry_Teenager:*
Oh. I'm sorry.

*Tall_Dark_Dangerous:*
It's cool. Listening to the music he loved is the closest I'll ever get to him. Although I would have loved Jim Morrison anyway, he was spectacularly good at being a rock star!

*Angry_Teenager:*
He was also a skilled pianist. Talented guy...

*Tall_Dark_Dangerous:*
I wish I'd been alive in the 60s, it must have been so free, so liberating. Don't you think?

*Angry_Teenager:*
Do you mean getting off your face on LSD?

*Tall_Dark_Dangerous:*

Ha ha no. Not interested in any of that. I don't even drink.

*Angry_Teenager:*
Maybe you should change your profile name to Tall_Dark_Sensible?

*Tall_Dark_Dangerous:*
Ha ha. I'm not always sensible...

*Angry_Teenager:*
What's the most dangerous thing you've done then?

*Tall_Dark_Dangerous:*
Eaten undercooked chicken. And once I stayed out 15 mins past my curfew.

*Angry_Teenager:*
Wow! Ferocious!

*Tall_Dark_Dangerous:*
I might look all hard, dark and menacing on the outside but I'm soft underneath really.

*Angry_Teenager:*
Like a boiled egg?

*Tall_Dark_Dangerous:*
Ha ha, couldn't you think of a nicer way to describe me? Also don't tell anyone. I'd prefer people to keep seeing me as mysterious and untamed as well as devastatingly handsome.

*Angry_Teenager:*
Untamed? Like a badger.

*Tall_Dark_Dangerous:*
A badger? Another fantastic analogy. I was thinking more like a wolf.

*Angry_Teenager:*
I'm watching a documentary in the background. It has badgers on it. Or I was, before I was rudely interrupted by my new stalker.

*Tall_Dark_Dangerous:*
Ha ha. Don't pretend you're not pleased.

*Angry_Teenager:*
I'm really not. So, you're a wolf? You travel in a pack?

*Tall_Dark_Dangerous:*
No, actually, I travel alone.

*Angry_Teenager:*
So not wolf-like at all then…

*Tall_Dark_Dangerous:*
Are you always this difficult? Lone wolf then. But definitely a wolf. Did you know, the wolf is a symbol of guardianship, loyalty, and spirit. They have the ability to make quick and firm emotional attachments, and they're excellent at trusting their own instincts. Thus they teach the rest of us to do the same, to trust our hearts and minds, and have control over our own lives.

*Angry_Teenager:*
Deep.

*Tall_Dark_Dangerous:*

What animal would you be?

*Angry_Teenager:*
Probably a black panther.

*Tall_Dark_Dangerous:*
The ghost of the jungle. Interesting. Explain...

*Angry_Teenager:*
Strength, speed, stamina, endurance, durability. Genius-level intellect. Lives a solitary life.

*Tall_Dark_Dangerous:*
And dangerous...

*Angry_Teenager:*
Most people think that, but it isn't true. Panthers only attack if they feel threatened, so if you leave them alone, they will leave you alone.

*Tall_Dark_Dangerous:*
Do you want me to leave you alone?

*Angry_Teenager:*
How did you tell?

*Tall_Dark_Dangerous:*
You're beguiling and enigmatic. It's one of the things I like about you. I do have to go though. I promised my Mum I'd watch a movie with her.

Angry_Teenager:
Boiled egg.

Tall_Dark_Dangerous:
You're going to like me, I know you will. I'm always right.
Meet me on the way to school tomorrow?

*Angry_Teenager:*
Well given we walk the same way to school, there's a good
chance we will meet...

*Tall_Dark_Dangerous:*
No, meet me, officially. 8:15, big gate at the graveyard. It's not
a question.

*Angry_Teenager:*
You're domineering?

*Tall_Dark_Dangerous:*
Would you like me to be domineering?

*Angry_Teenager:*
I'm going...

*Tall_Dark_Dangerous:*
Ok. See you by the gate. Don't be late. Oh, and Kya?

*Angry_Teenager:*
?

*Tall_Dark_Dangerous:*
Please wear the red lipstick :-)

## Kya

I close my laptop. Did that conversation actually just happen? I'm feeling slightly flushed, and my heart seems to be beating faster than usual. No, this is not happening. I am not going to get involved. I don't even know him. He's probably some weirdo loner. Anyway, getting involved with anyone is not on my agenda. Focusing on my studies so I can get the hell out of here is. I look up the definition of beguiling – *charming or enchanting*. My heart flutters a little. I tell myself not to start going soft. Enigmatic – *difficult to interpret and understand*. That's good, keep him guessing. Wait, no, I don't want him guessing! I am not going down that road. I lie back on my bed and try to go to sleep. Why can't I stop thinking about him?

## Zak

I can't stop thinking about her. I wanted to chat all night but I also wanted to play it cool, I don't want to scare her off. I re-read our conversation and smile. God, she's alluring. I look up the word alluring to check it has the right meaning – *powerfully and mysteriously attractive or fascinating, seductive*. Yes, she is most definitely alluring. But there's something else, something I can't quite put my finger on. Something I know she's not going to let me see. Why was she crying in the graveyard that day? She's not the fluffy type who would cry at anything. It must be big. I want to be the one she lets in. I lie back on my bed and try to fall asleep. Kya is such a beautiful name. Distinctive, individual, mysterious, just like her.

## Kya

I wake up and my first thought is of him, the boy in black, or Zak as I now know he's called. Zak, I like that name, it's rockstarish. I lie in bed and try to piece together the remnants of last night's dreams, a crazy mash-up of scenes, me walking through the graveyard to school, then me running away from someone through thick dense forest and thorny bushes, the hummingbird in the bell jar, desperately trying to escape before it perishes. And he's always there in the background, dressed all in black, silent, watching me. It was strangely comforting him being there. I try to make sense of this feeling I have in my stomach and I realise with part joy part horror what it is – I ache to see him. I try to visualise his face in my mind but I can't, no matter how hard I try, all I can see is black hair flopping over a featureless face. Does he have pale skin? What colour are his eyes? Why am I drawn to him in such a peculiar way? I can't picture his face at all. What if I meet him and he's nothing like I'm imagining? He might be a wacko or a contemptible pervert. That would be disappointing. These odd yet heated feelings have sprung up from nowhere, and although I'm trying to suppress them, they're definitely there.

I take slightly longer getting ready this morning. I'm not usually overly concerned about my hair and makeup but I find myself giving it extra attention today. *Oh, and Kya? Please wear the red lipstick!* The words go round and round my head as I carefully apply the colour to my lips. He likes the red. I like the red. Not because I'm trying to be sexy, or make a statement, it's just me.

I always try to stay in my room until the last minute so I spend as little time as possible around *him* in the morning. He hasn't spoken to me much this past week which is a blessing, he just throws disapproving looks my way or spits out some disparaging remark or scornful comment over dinner. But I can handle the bitter sting of his spiteful words. They're just words. And I can handle him trying to make me feel like an outsider to their perfect little family unit, or the way he tries to turn Lizzie away from me. He hates that me and Lizzie are so close, and feels he has to regularly remind me what a *negative influence* I am on her. Then he reminds Lizzie that *your sister's not the kind of girl you'll turn out like, Elizabeth.* Just words. And I can handle words. As long as he doesn't come anywhere near me.

I hear the childminder's car pull up so I leave my room and run down the stairs.

'Kya!' Lizzie runs up to me and throws her arms around my legs. I crouch down to her level and give her the biggest squeeze ever. She pulls back and studies my face. 'Kya, you look pretty!'

'Thank you, baby girl, so do you!'

She laughs, and I try to ignore him scowling at me.

'That is not pretty, Elizabeth, that is what you call *unbefitting*.' He looks at me with abhorrence.

'Oh.' Lizzie looks sad, confused.

35

'*You're* pretty, Elizabeth,' he smiles his sickly smile at her as he picks her up to take her outside to the childminder. 'And you will never need to wear that disgusting makeup, will you, angel?'

Lizzie looks at me and smiles, but it doesn't reach her eyes. She looks sad, and I wonder what all this does to her. I want to say *bye!* as she's carried out of the door but the lump in my throat is so big I know if I speak it will come out as a sob, so I do a big fake smile and wave enthusiastically instead.

## Lizzie

'Daddy, why did you call Kya not pretty? I think Kya is pretty.' He puts me down on the ground and he's squeezing my hand a bit too tight as he takes me to Katy who looks after me.

'Because, my angel, Kya is disgraceful, and I don't want you growing up like her.' He is whispering but he sounds cross.

'But why? Owww!' he's pulling my arm.

'Because she's not like you, angel, that's why. You must always remember that.'

He says hello to Katy and they strap me into my car seat.

'Ok, well have a great day, angel!'

'Bye, Daddy.'

'What do you say?' He does that thing where he talks quietly but I know he's cross really.

'You're the best daddy in the world and I love you.'

'Good girl, Daddy loves you too, angel.'

We drive off and I wave at him but I feel a bit sick in my tummy. I still think Kya is pretty.

## Kya

I'm livid. I want to ask him why he thinks it's ok to try and turn my little sister away from me. But I can't, obviously, because it will start a fight, and I just want to get out of the house quickly, and unscathed, this morning. I butter my toast as quickly as I can. He comes back in. I don't look up, but I can feel the atmosphere change. He bustles noisily around the kitchen, slamming things down and sighing heavily, and I know he's angry, spoiling for a fight. If I keep quiet, I might just get out. I grab a banana, slice of toast in the other hand, and head for the kitchen door.

'So, you think it's appropriate to parade yourself around looking like a harlot, do you?'

And there it is.

I ignore him and grab my coat but he follows me into the hall.

'Answer me?' He says it like it's a question. I just glare at him, too angry to say anything. Too afraid to say anything, which in turn makes me angrier still.

'I SAID, do you think it's appropriate to parade yourself around looking like a harlot?'

'I'm not parading myself around.' I keep my eyes on the ground as I put my coat on. *Stay calm, just get out of here.*

'So the black eyeliner, the red lipstick, you think that's befitting for a girl your age?'

'I'm sixteen.'

'You look like a common little slut.'

I ignore him as I zip up my bag and swing it over my shoulder, which clearly incenses him.

'And do you think it's a good example to set Elizabeth?' He never refers to her as my sister. 'Do not ignore me, young lady.'

'What do you want me to say?'

'Do you want Elizabeth turning out like you?'

*Well I hope to God she doesn't turn out like you!* I want to scream. 'I'm going to school.'

I continue to avoid his stare, and it's taking every ounce of self-control I have not to burst into tears or burst into a rage, though I know his face has taken on that familiar shade of red, and I know without looking that his mouth will be puckered up, and his eyes will be burning with wrath.

'You are *not* going out looking like that.' And with that, he grabs my arm and yanks me back, and before I know it his hand is smearing the lipstick off my face. I struggle to break free but he is stronger than me. I can smell his bitter coffee breath as he grips my arm tighter and his big hands and thick fingers repeatedly rub my mouth. Saliva flies out of his mouth and onto my face as he spits words out between clenched teeth, something about *Bringing shame on the family* and *What would people think* and *How does it look when a councillor's step-daughter looks like a slattern.*

'Get *OFF!*' I manage to break free and run for the door, and he lets me go. I slam the door behind me and run to the end of my road, not stopping for breath until I've rounded the corner. I slump back against a wall and fight harder than I've ever fought to keep the angry tears away, to stop myself from screaming out loud, to stop myself from pummeling the wall with my fists. But I keep it in, just. I've become good at it, swallowing the persecution, swallowing it down like a bitter pill. But the thing about pain, anger, rage, resentment – it needs a place to go, and if it doesn't come out, it has to stay inside. But how long can it stay inside for? I imagine the toxic loathing pervading my body, destroying my cells, blackening my heart, disintegrating all that is good. I check my watch, it's 8:15am. *Not now,* I tell myself, *push it away for now.* I take a few deep breaths to steady myself and I feel my heart rate slowing. I'm determined not to *feel* right now. I won't let him beat me down. I take out my pocket mirror and almost laugh at what I look like, red lipstick smeared around my mouth, looking like the Joker. I'm thankful for the small makeup bag I keep in my school rucksack, and within a few minutes I've fixed my face. I give myself an extra lick of black eyeliner as a token of defiance and I reapply my *Red Rebellion* lipstick carefully. As I put my mirror back in my pocket, I say the words out loud, as if they'll somehow reach him – *Fuck. You.*

## Kya

'You're late,' he says.

'You're unrelenting.'

'You're wearing the red lipstick,' he notes.

'I always wear it. It's not for you.'

He smiles, 'You're a closed book.'

I look at him, and as our eyes meet I feel that peculiar feeling again. I'm relieved to realise I'm not disappointed; on the contrary, I am mesmerised by his face. His angular features, his cheekbones and his pronounced jawline, softened by his floppy dark hair framing his face. He brushes it aside to reveal the deepest, darkest eyes I've ever seen. As we look at each other it feels like he is staring deep into my soul. I break the stare. I don't want anyone to see into my soul.

'We'd better get going,' I say.

We fall into step, and I can feel how tall he is beside me. Tall and lean. Protective. I think of what he said about the wolf – *a symbol of guardianship*.

'So, you're in year 11?' he says, slowing his pace slightly to let me keep up.

'Yeah, the final stretch. And I'm guessing you're in sixth form, but I never saw you around school before this year?'

'I moved here at the start of the year. My mum has sisters here. She wanted to wait until I'd finished school. She thought starting a new college wouldn't be as bad as leaving halfway through school.'

He looks down at the ground and lets his hair cover his eyes – almost looking shifty. I sense he's not telling me everything.

'And was it? OK? Starting over I mean.'

'It was fine. I wasn't attached to my old place. I mean, I had friends and all, but I kind of welcomed the new start. And I like it here. Plus this place has a better philosophy course.'

'Philosophy? Interesting. I'm taking it next year.'

'Really? I had a feeling we would have plenty in common.' He grins down at me, a self-assured but very sexy grin, a bit of mischief in his eyes. I push that thought away.

'Philosophy, English Literature and English Language,' I say, steering the conversation back to safe ground.

'Wow, we really are similar! I knew we would be.'

'You're soft,' I say.

'You're mystifying,' he grins.

I smile back. I quite like being unfathomable, and the thought that someone wants to fathom me out, well, it's new to me, and I quite like it. We talk comfortably, and I realise I'm enjoying the company. There's something about him. He makes me feel relaxed and calm.

We get to school and there's an awkward moment, like he doesn't want to part. I'm not sure I want to, either. I feel a certain magnetism between us which unnerves me slightly.

'So, I'll see you later then?' he says.

'We go to the same school. We walk the same route. Odds are you will.' I want to be nicer but I'm so used to being

42

glacial. He smiles at me. It's like me being unforthcoming makes him like me more.

'Later,' I confirm, smiling coyly, giving him something, and I look in his eyes for a second longer than I mean to, before I turn and walk away.

'Later,' I hear him say, and I know he's not moving. I don't look back, but I know he's standing there watching me walk away. And the strange thing is, I like him watching me.

# Zak

8:30am. I wasn't sure if she would turn up. She seems harried, like she's carrying some sort of mental or emotional strain. I'm good at reading people. Has she been crying? I desperately want her to let me in, but I'm not sure she's the type to share her feelings easily. She's guarded, defensive. This only makes me want her more. I want her to believe in love and destiny like I do, but right now she looks like she would tear someone apart limb from limb rather than let them read poetry to her. I believe in fate, and the universe conspiring to bring two people together. She believes in *'you make your own destiny'*. We talk about school and how she's studying hard for her exams. Thankfully she's staying on at college and is taking Philosophy, so I know she's a great thinker like me. She asks why I moved here and I tell her it's so Mum can be closer to her sisters, which is partly true, but it's not the entire truth. I can't tell her the real reason we had to move here. I can't exactly tell her what I did, she'd run a mile. She reads a lot and I tell her reading is sexy. She blushes slightly at this which endears her to me. I've never met a girl who is into The Doors, and she's into Nietzsche! We have so much in common and I'm pretty sure we could talk all day. The magnetism between us is palpable, and I know, the *universe* knows, that we're meant to be together.

We're about to say goodbye at school and she looks at me and I'm sure she's thinking what I'm thinking. I know she has barriers, but for a moment I see through them and I could get lost in her eyes. There is so much inside there. So much to her. If only she'd let me in. I'm going to prove to her she can trust me. I watch her walk away. She can't see me watching her, so I stand and stare longer than I probably should. I steal a long look at her legs. Slim, shapely, sexy in her black tights. For a second I imagine her naked, her pale, creamy skin, then a flush of guilt snaps me back to reality. This isn't just about physical attraction. This is more than that. This is deep. An undeniable connection, and I know it's there. I go to my first lesson and my thoughts are occupied by naked pale skin, emerald green eyes, red lips and raven black hair.

## Kya

I can't focus today, my mind is all over the place. I try not to think of this morning at home, but my thoughts keep flashing back to what he said to Lizzie about me not being pretty. I know I always say *They're just words* and *Words can't hurt me* but this time his words have hit as hard as his fist, and it's left a mark, like a scar, prominent and red and ugly. Eventually it will fade and become less noticeable, but it will never fully disappear. I have plenty of scars, they're just on the inside.

I run my hand over my sleeve and it feels tender where he grabbed my wrist. I'll probably have a bruise and it won't be the first time. I sometimes think it would be easier if he just beat me up and did a proper job of it, leaving a swollen black eye or a cracked rib or something, then I'd have substantial proof and I might even be able to do something about it. Maybe Mum would do something about it then, or the police. I can't exactly report him for calling me names. I wonder if he does it on purpose, doing just enough to make my life a misery, but not quite enough for anyone to sit up and take notice.

The persecution is harsh and unrelenting in matters big and small, and the persistent undercurrent of abusive behaviour is taking its toll, becoming harder to bear. The humiliation, the constant criticism, the threats, the shouting, the name calling, the blaming, the scapegoating, the insults. Trying to alienate me from Mum, the constant comparisons between me and Lizzie. Yelling, screaming, the venomous jibes that serve to make me feel small and inconsequential. Belittling any type of accomplishments like getting straight A's at school each year – *That's hardly an achievement.* Or trying to claim responsibility for said accomplishments – *You wouldn't be at that school if it wasn't for me, paying for this house in a nice area. Where would you and your mother be if it wasn't for me?* The derogatory names, which aren't really terms of endearment, they're just wrapped up as affectionate pet names like *The Troublesome Teenager,* which he uses when he's playing the perfect step-dad in front of the neighbours, or the various work colleagues that come for dinner. He'll make me the butt of jokes and try to make me look foolish in front of them, and if I dare to object, he'll claim to be teasing, tell me I haven't got a sense of humour. He'll roll his eyes in an exasperated way and say *Told you, moody teenager!* and everyone will laugh and know me as the wayward problematic teenager, when actually he's the cause of all my indignation. He's good at turning the tables too – goading then blaming. He'll go out of his way to taunt me, then once the trouble starts, it's my fault for creating it; I've caused his rage, if I wasn't so problematic he wouldn't have to assert his authority, and so it goes on. Then there's the character assassination. This usually involves the word *always. You're always going against our core family values, you're always disagreeable, you're always setting a bad example to Lizzie,* and so on. Basically, he's constantly affirming I'm not a good person, and trying to undermine my self-esteem. I think he hopes if he says it enough I'll start to believe it myself. But I won't let him break me.

These thoughts clutter my head and are mingled with thoughts of Zak. *Zak*. I say his name over and over in my head. I wonder what he'd think if he knew I've only had one boyfriend before, and even that didn't last. I liked him, but I didn't love him. I think that's when I realised I was different to my friends, well, my friends at the time, when they started becoming interested in boys.

One day we were interested in ourselves and our lives and the world around us and then boom, overnight nothing else mattered but boys. They became obsessed with the opposite sex. Then they started dating, and the whole world revolved around their boyfriends, and I was expected to be as interested as they were. I never understood why they would go all mushy and in love. I eventually followed suit and I got a boyfriend, not that I was actively looking. He pursued me and I was a bit like whatever, I may as well, it's what everyone else is doing – what *I'm* supposed to be doing. It was pleasant enough. I'd just turned fifteen and I liked the feeling of being like a normal teenager – going on double dates on a Friday night, but I never felt those all-encompassing feelings that my friends seemed to feel. I never felt giddy or weak at the knees. I mean, I liked him. He was good looking, and I liked looking at him, and I liked to kiss him. But I didn't *need* him, and I never got how the girls that were once so strong and independent with thoughts and opinions of their own were suddenly all *I can't live without him*, and cry for weeks when it ended. *You can't live without him?* I'd think. *Then why aren't you dead yet?*

Anyway, it wasn't long before his typical boy traits shone through and it was clear what he was after. We were at a party and he suggested we go into another room. We'd kissed before, but the way he was kissing me this time was different, in a disagreeable way. It felt off. This wasn't about me, or love, or feeling, it was simply about scoring, and about having something to tell his mates afterwards. As soon as he put his hands up my jumper and I felt them on my bare skin I freaked out. He called me frigid, stormed out of the room and never spoke to me again. I'm not sure I'll ever be able to be intimate with a guy. I don't want anyone getting that close to me. I don't ever want to want or need a guy or depend on anyone. I don't want to be like Mum. I will be independent and will never be used or controlled by anyone. Ever.

I'm dreading going home, thank the stars Mum's not working tonight. My mind starts to quiet and my rampant thoughts are slowing down. I can't let any of this, *him* or Zak, distract me from my school work, it's far too important. I don't need anyone or anything, but I do need to get my final grades at the end of term, get through the next two years of college and get into a university a long way away from here.

## Zak

We didn't arrange to meet after school, but I make sure I run out of my last class quickly and wait by the school gate. We walk home the same way, so it's not like I'm being forward, just practical. I spot her a mile off, in amongst the sea of high school and college students. She hasn't seen me yet, so I watch her intently. Girls skip past her, giggling, pouting, swishing their hair, probably talking about meaningless drivel. She's a world away from them, unlike anyone else, special. She's about average height, slim, but not skinny. Under her clothes I know she'll have curves in all the right places. She doesn't want to be in the spotlight, doesn't need to be popular, or seen, but she knows who she is, has a certain strength about her. As she walks, she looks calm, collected, self-assured. Her black hair falls just past her shoulders, flicking out to the sides. Then she sees me. Something inside me stirs, and for a moment I'm anxious. Will she be mad? She's looking at me fixedly as she walks towards me, and I can't read her.

'You waiting for someone?' Her face softens slightly as she reaches me. She knows I'm waiting for her.

'Might be.' I smile. She smiles back, in her own reserved way, and starts walking. We fall into step comfortably and she seems much more relaxed than she was this morning as she talks about her classes. It's incredible the way she sparkles when she talks about something she's passionate about. It's clear she's devoted to her studies, especially literature.

'So what's been the most interesting part of your day?' she asks.

'Philosophy class of course. We're studying Nietzsche.'

'Ah, the great German philosopher. Is it true he embraced nihilism and rejected all philosophical reasoning?'

'Some say so. Others say that in an attempt to thwart the predicted rise of nihilism, he looked at other ways to reaffirm life, and called for a radical, naturalistic rethinking of the nature of human existence. He was all for *becoming what one is* or the creation of self through the cultivation of instincts, crafting one's own identity through self-realisation, with no reliance on anything transcending life.'

'Anything transcending life?'

'Yeh, like God, or a soul.'

'Surely that conflicts with some people's psychological and intellectual inheritances? I mean, a lot of people believe in God.'

'Yeah, a lot of people still question the coherence of his views, although his ideas have often been seized upon and twisted by readers. Have you read anything of his?'

'I've read *Human, All-Too Human.*'

'One of his least romantic texts.'

'I've got *The Will to Power* at home. It's on my ever expanding *to be read* pile.'

I'm captivated by her. I could talk with her all day. Her eyes light up when she's talking about philosophy or literature, the intensity of her emotions, her fervour, brimming over. I watch her red lips move as she speaks. We're lost in conversation when we reach the gate at the end of the graveyard. We stop and face each other. I don't want to part company. She looks at me and I sense she's feeling the same. I look into her eyes and for a moment I feel like she's letting her barriers down, her eyes are open and accepting, inviting even, and she lets me stare in wonderment at them, and it's then I notice the colour changing and taking on a deeper emerald hue. Then she looks away, the windows to her soul no longer open.

'So,' I say.

'So…'

'What do you usually do after school?' I want to keep the conversation going for as long as possible, so we don't have to say goodbye.

'Oh, you know, I'm really busy with extracurricular activities – cheerleading club, ballet, cooking class and hanging out with my girlfriends talking about makeup and boys.'

I know she's being sardonic and there's a cheeky glint in her eye. I laugh.

'I haven't known you long but I do know that would be your worst nightmare!'

She laughs too, her red lips parting and revealing straight, white teeth, and for a moment she looks free. Free from whatever it is she's carrying around.

'So really, what do you do?'

'Not much I guess. I study. I read. I look after my little sister Lizzie when my mum's working nights at the care home. Listen to music a lot.

'What kind of music are you into?'

'I'm quite into Tortured Heart at the moment, you heard of them?'

'Yeh, are they that American rock band? Or is it metal, or grunge?'

'I don't know if I'm honest, maybe alternative metal, gothic rock? I'm not usually into rock as such, but I like them, they're dark and twisty, and I like her, the lead singer. She does things her way.'

I make a mental note to listen to them later.

'So what else do you do?' I ask.

'That's it really, unless I have a break in routine when a stalker contacts me on messenger.'

The way she looks at me when she says this, playfully, I feel something stir inside me. I want to reach out and stroke the pastel skin on her cheek, move her inky black hair out of her face with my fingers and feel its softness.

'You're staring at me again.'

She says it in almost a hushed tone, having lost the icy tone she had this morning, and this time she doesn't break eye contact. Her eyes are on mine, intense, and I have the feeling she'll keep them there until I answer. I pause, enjoying the intensity as long as I can.

'I can't help it, there's something about you,' I say, almost whispering, hypnotized. She lets me keep staring. Her eyes are telling me something. *I want you too.* For a moment I imagine kissing her, leaning forward until my lips are on hers, soft and red. Taking her into my arms and running my hands through her hair as our kissing becomes more urgent.

'You're blushing,' she teases. Vision gone, thankfully, back to reality. I consider denying it for a brief second but then think better of it. I think about covering it up with something funny but it would be insincere. Instead, I choose to wear my heart on my sleeve and be honest.

'When I look into your eyes I tend to lose my thoughts. You have honest eyes, like they would always tell the truth, even if your mouth was telling a lie. There's a light in them that speaks to me louder than words.'

She's silent, she looks at me and for a moment I see her vulnerability, her eyes glistening, like I've touched her soul.

Then the barriers are back, her defences return and she tries to lighten the mood.

'Were you having improper thoughts about me?' She's teasing me again, deflecting from the openness of my emotions. Is she flirting? I can see a mischievous gleam in her eye. Damn she's sexy. I think for a moment what her reaction would be if I told her the truth. *Yes, I was, I was imagining taking your hand and leading you over there, behind that enormous tree. I'd pull you close to me, stare into your eyes for a moment before leaning in and kissing your beautiful red lips. I'd kiss you passionately, and push you back gently against the tree, letting my hands wander over your body, feeling the shape of you through your clothes…*

'Oh my God you were!' she laughs. 'You're blushing again!'

I put my hands up in the air in mock surrender and smile innocently, hoping she doesn't think I'm a total pervert. She doesn't seem bothered by my silent admission of inappropriate thoughts. If I know her, which I think I do, she's actually enjoying it.

'Well, don't get carried away,' she's being serious now. 'I'm off the market.'

My heart plummets.

'Oh, sorry, I er,' I'm lost for words, 'I didn't realise you had a boyfriend.'

'I don't.'

My hopes lift again, but then, shit, maybe she has a girlfriend!

'I'm just not in a position to get involved with anyone.'

Phew, no girlfriend. But still, shit.

I look at her silently, urging her to elaborate.

'I'm too busy. And I need to focus on school. I can't have any distractions. I don't want anyone being all needy and demanding of me. I haven't got anything to give anyone right now anyway.'

My heart sinks, but I know the stars are aligning for us, and I'm happy to be patient.

'Well, I'd settle for being good friends, if you'll have me?'

She looks at me, and for a moment I think she might cry. There's a sadness in her eyes now, and weirdly her eyes become even more beautiful when they're wet. I can see her pain, almost feel it. *What the hell is causing it?*

'I won't make a very good friend.' Barriers back up. Ice Queen front applied. Mask on.

'Oh really? I find that hard to believe?'

'I'm impatient, insolent, unfeeling, and unforgiving.' She looks at me sternly, as if to prove she's as hard as she's describing, but I see through the act.

'I'm not afraid of your darkness, Kya.'

She looks at me, stunned. I've pierced the armour.

'There's a bed of roses under there,' I move a step forward, closing the gap between us, 'and there's no beautiful surface without a terrible depth.'

'You're quoting Nietzsche,' she half laughs, quietly, holding my gaze.

'I told you, I'm a bit of a romantic,' I say quietly, staring into her eyes, not wanting this moment to end.

'There's no bed of roses with me, Zak, just thorns.'

'I'm not afraid of thorns either. When I find something this beautiful, I'll do my best to hold onto it, even if there are thorns in my path. I'll cut them down or walk right through them if I have to.'

Her eyes are wet with tears now, and despite my reservations I do what's natural – I reach forward and take her hand. She lets me. It's gloriously soft, and despite her cold demeanour it's warm. I imagine the blood under her skin, the same colour as her lips. She looks down at my hand and for a moment I think she's going to pull away, but she doesn't. She looks at my face, and her eyes flicker to my lips. I glance at hers, blood red, full, wanting. God those lips. Every fibre in my body aches to lean forward and kiss her. It would be the most natural thing in the world, but I've already come this far with her and I don't want to ruin it. Not here, not now. I want to wait, to show her I'm not just about making out. Show her it's important to me too, for everything to be at the right time.

A reluctant tear escapes and rolls down her cheek. I move my hand slowly, so slowly, so as not to surprise her, and I'm astonished that she stands stock still, knowing what I'm going to do, and I reach up and wipe it away gently with my finger. I've dreamed about touching her cheek, so pale, the colour of cream, and it feels even better than I'd imagined, soft as cashmere, and not cool, but warm. She has love in there, so much love. She's not an ice queen, she yearns to be touched, to be held, to be protected.

'What are you afraid of, Kya?'

'I'm flawed.' Her voice cracks slightly, and it takes everything I have not to just grab her and hold her in my arms. I squeeze her hand gently, I never want to let go.

'We are all inevitably flawed. But you, you are beautifully flawed. Perfectly imperfect, and beautifully flawed.'

She smiles at me and it's as if our souls meet. I know right then and there she feels the same.

## Kya

I don't want to say goodbye when we reach the gate. And not just because I'm dreading going home, but because I don't want to leave him. I'm paralysed by his stare. He is captivating – crazy-intelligent, funny, self-assured, and he remains unperturbed by my constant rebuffing. We talk about school and I find it so easy. I feel like I've known him my whole life. He's staring at me again. I stare back at him intensely. Am I flirting?

'You're staring at me again.'

'I can't help it, there's something about you,' he almost whispers. I hold his gaze, enjoying the power I seem to hold over him. *I want you too*, I think. For a moment I think he's going to kiss me. In that moment I *want* him to kiss me. *Just let him*, I tell myself. He stares at my mouth and I wait for him to make a move. He holds back, his mind elsewhere. I notice he's blushing. I tease him. I feel a certain carnal power and I relish it. I decide to wind him up, asking him if he's having improper thoughts. He doesn't admit it but he doesn't deny it either.

Strangely, I am pleased by this. I'm enjoying the thought

of him thinking about me like that, wanting me, needing me. But I need to snap out of it. *Stop it.* I tell him I'm off the market and I see the disappointment cloud his face. I feel a flash of guilt but I have to stay strong, remember, I have to look after myself. I'm genuine when I say I've got nothing to give. He says he's happy to be friends, but I can't deny it, I want more. Why can't I give more? I feel a sadness rise up within me so I do what I do best, I put my barriers up, ice queen mask on. I rebuff him again. He remains undeterred and quotes Nietzsche, *There is no beautiful surface without a terrible depth.* His romanticism mixed with a dash of bad boy is sexy. He steps forward and I'm surprised I don't automatically move back to maintain the space between us, and instead remain rooted to the spot. I'm trying desperately not to cry, the sadness and fear is welling up inside me and it has no place to go. He reaches forward and takes my hand, and in the exact moment his skin touches mine, I feel the electricity between us. I consider pulling away, instinct, but I'm powerless in his presence. His hand feels strong, protective, and despite how big it is, it fits perfectly with mine. I look at his face, his angular features. He is stunning. I look at his lips, so drawn to them, and I yearn for him to press them to mine. I sense he doesn't want to come on strong and I like him even more for that. I'm mortified when a tear escapes. I've never let anyone see me vulnerable, it's not me. He gestures slowly to reach up and wipe it away and I let him, enjoying the feel of his hand on my cheek, the electricity jolting through me again. I want to close my eyes and lose myself in his touch. *What are you afraid of, Kya?* he breathes, his dark eyes looking at me intensely.

*What am I afraid of?* I don't know where to start. When you put the barriers up and close yourself off to pain, you close yourself off to love. You can't close one and keep the other open, it doesn't work like that. So if I open myself up to feel love, I also have to open up the part of me that also feels pain. And that's too scary. It's easier to keep it all locked up. Self-preservation. I have a world of pain inside me and a torrent of anger. How do I summarise that? I keep it simple and tell him simply, I'm flawed. I could use a thousand words to detail exactly what I'm afraid of and why I am no good for him, but I use just two words. He squeezes my hand gently and this time the electricity runs all through my body. I never want him to let go. *We are all inevitably flawed. But you, you are beautifully flawed. Perfectly imperfect, and beautifully flawed.* To know I am beautiful in his eyes makes me feel beautiful and whole. I haven't felt whole since I don't know when. I smile at him and it's as if our souls connect. I wonder, if he looked into my eyes long enough, would he see what's inside?

## Zak

We leave the graveyard and I walk her home. We don't hold hands, but we walk close enough that we keep brushing each other's arms. She lives only a street away from me. The closer we get the more she stiffens up. She won't let me walk her all the way, and insists on me leaving her at the corner, and I wonder what it is behind those walls that she's hiding. She seems reluctant to go home. We say goodbye, and after I've watched her walk away and through her front door, I walk home slowly, pondering the meaning of love, and wondering what she's so afraid of. I wonder what is causing the pain she is so evidently carrying around with her. I wonder why a girl who seems to have so much passion inside her, is so unwilling to acknowledge emotions or consider love? She doesn't want to show her vulnerabilities. She said she doesn't want to get hurt, doesn't want to depend on anyone, and I wonder what makes people so afraid of themselves, so afraid of their reality, so afraid of their feelings. People fear pain, and hurt. Love can be painful. It can hurt, yes. But I truly believe you'll never feel the depth, the wonder, the power of love if you're not willing to take the risk and feel some pain.

I get home and head straight to my room. I don't even switch my music on, even that will interrupt my thoughts of her, and I want to be alone with these thoughts, as I lie on my bed. I can't help these feelings towards her. I want her so much. The chemistry I feel when we're together, it's intoxicating. Clearly there's a part of me that is just like any other horny seventeen-year-old guy, and although I'm more than that, *that* part of me can't stop thinking about her. Her legs in those black tights with those boots. I imagine feeling the soft silkiness of her tights as I run my hands up under her skirt. If I let my imagination run too wild, I think about ripping those tights... And her red lips... I think about what they would feel like against mine. Warm, full, inviting. I imagine her kissing me harder, biting my bottom lip, then moving onto my neck, kissing, licking, biting softly, tantalizing. I start to think of her red lips kissing places where I ache for her lips to go, and I have to stop myself sharp. For all her steely exterior she is delicate. She is special. She is not a piece of meat. I switch off those thoughts, the *horny seventeen-year-old-guy* thoughts. I know the day will come. She will fall in love with me, like I love her already. It will be the kind of love neither of us ever expected. A love so powerful and all-encompassing we will be powerless to resist it. I will stare into her eyes and still believe they are the most beautiful in the whole world. She will look back at me like she's just realised I'm the one, and the light in her eyes will say *I'm yours*, like I'm everything she needs. She'll look at me with knowing in her eyes, because finally, she understands. *Be patient*, I tell myself, *and learn to wait*. There is beauty in waiting. Although it can be a desolate time, and I ache for her, life continues to be beautiful. I only have to look up at the stars to remind me that they are still shining for us. It will come. Just be patient. After all, it's the patient person who receives the best love story. Just as long as she doesn't find out my secret and run a mile.

## Kya

Mum and Lizzie are already home. I can hear Mum in the kitchen and Lizzie's watching TV in the living room so I go to her first. She's sitting cross legged on the floor rug humming along to the theme tune of her favourite cartoon.

'Kya!' She gets up and runs over to me and hugs my legs. She's always so pleased to see me, and I sometimes feel like she's the only person in the world that truly loves me. I know Mum loves me, but Lizzie loves me unconditionally. She doesn't get frustrated with me, or resent me for not getting on with her husband, or for not just keeping quiet and brushing things under the carpet so we can pretend to be one big happy family like she wants it to be. I know she loves me, but I can feel Mum's bitter indignation towards me, and sometimes that can hurt more than a punch in the stomach or a bruised wrist. They're emotional wounds, the kind that never show on the body but are deeper and more painful than anything that bleeds. Lizzie pulls my arm and I join her on the rug.

'What are we watching, baby girl?'

'Frankie and Fuzzy!'

'I *love* Frankie and Fuzzy!' I say animatedly, in the voice of a big fuzzy bear, and Lizzie laughs and snuggles into my lap and I kiss the top of her blonde curls. Her hair smells like strawberry shampoo. She's one of the reasons I keep going. I love her with every fibre of my being, and will do whatever it takes to protect her. Mum calls me into the kitchen and reluctantly I get up and go in.

'Hey.' I know she knows about this morning, because he comes home for his lunch every day and will have already told her his version of events. I am hostile towards her already because I know what's coming.

'I heard about the ruckus this morning.'

'Ruckus? Oh, you mean your husband calling me a slut and a harlot and accusing me of being a bad example to my sister? Who, by the way *is* my sister, despite the fact *he* can't stand it and would have us genetically separated if he could.'

'Why are you so angry, Kya? If you could just…'

'*Angry?*' I shout, exasperated. I can feel the furious tears pushing at the back of my eyeballs. 'The fact that you can't even see why I could possibly be angry, or upset, or hurt,' I pull up my sleeve and show her the bruise on my wrist. She looks at it and for a second I see the shock and hurt in her eyes, the mum I once knew, the mum who would've thrown herself in front of a train for me, the mum who wiped my tears and lay with me and stroked my hair all night if I was poorly, the mum who marched up to school when Sally Wilson made my life a misery in preschool. But that look quickly disappears. It's easier for her to just pretend it's all a big fuss over nothing.

'Why do you have to antagonize him? Can't you just…'

'*Antagonise* him? Mum, can you see this fucking bruise?' I am bewildered beyond belief.

'Kya,' she sighs like this is all a big misunderstanding and I'm overreacting and once again *I'm* causing the problem here.

'No, Mum. I can't take this anymore. Why won't you stand up to him? Stand up for *me*? Why won't you admit that what he's doing is wrong? So wrong! I shouldn't have to live like this!' I'm shouting now, and tears of anger and frustration and hurt and despair are running black tracks of mascara down my face. I want to scream and shout and pound the kitchen worktop and smash everything in sight.

'This is difficult for me, Kya.'

'Difficult for *you*? Mum, you *choose* to be with him! You choose him over me, time after time!'

'Why do you always do that? Why do you always have to put me in the middle?'

And there it is. The relinquishing of responsibility. *I* put her in the middle, *I* do this to her, none of this is her fault, she's the victim.

'Oh great, so now I'm the one at fault here?' I'm not even surprised. I've been here a hundred times before. I'm wasting my breath.

'If you could just…'

'If I could just what, Mum? Be more of a perfect daughter? Hey? What does that look like to you? If I could just pull my weight around the house? Oh hang on a minute, *I do*! If I could just work hard at school, stay out of trouble, get perfect grades? Oh wait, *I DO!*'

'You're blowing this all out of proportion honey, now come on, calm down.'

'Mum, he makes my life a misery! He *lives* for making my life a misery, and he gets off on it! Can't you see that?'

'He's a good man underneath.'

'Underneath what? The starched shirts that you meticulously iron for him because you're basically his maid? He is what he is, Mum, and he gets away with it because he's a *respected member of the community* and everyone admires him, with his phoney smile and charm. But it's all fake! He's a bully and a control freak and I fucking hate him!'

'Kya! He does a lot for us! Where would we be without him, hey? You two just clash. You're both as hot headed and stubborn as each other.'

'We *clash*? Mum, he torments me. Have you heard yourself? You're deluded. Can't you see how he treats you even? You have no say, no authority, he makes all the decisions. Christ, you haven't even got access to your joint bank account, where *your* wages go. You have to ask him for money if you need something, and even then you have to account for every penny you spend.'

'Stop exaggerating,' she laughs weakly, 'you make things sound much worse than they are. I'm happy for him to be in charge of the bills, that's his role, and you know I hate doing all that stuff.'

'But you have no say! You have no control at all! And you've lost your identity, Mum. You've traded your soul, and for what? So you don't have to worry about the gas bill?'

I'm talking normally now, I've no energy left for yelling. We sit at the kitchen table but she won't look me in the eye. I know that somewhere, somewhere in there she knows the truth, knows that what I'm saying is right. Why is it so hard for her to admit it and do something about it?

'You're not allowed out during the day, you have to be here for his lunch,' I say softly, because despite how she refuses to protect me, I love her more than anything else in the world and I feel sorry for her.

She laughs quietly, brushing it off. 'I choose to be home during the day. He's my husband Kya, of course I want to be home with him.'

'You're *expected* to be home during the day, Mum.

Remember those girly days we used to have in the school holidays? You used to panic if you were going to be late back to get his lunch, because he expected his lunch on the table at a certain time and God forbid if you weren't there to wait on him. His lunch soon became more important than our time together. And eventually, the girly days stopped altogether.'

She looks at the table. She knows it's the truth, but it hurts too much to acknowledge it, so it's easier to deny it. She looks affronted, and infuriatingly, I know she feels the unfair treatment is coming from me, not him. This maddens me and hurts me in equal measure but I carry on, speaking even more softly now. Maybe she'll actually take it in if she doesn't feel like she's being told off.

'You don't see your friends anymore…'

'I don't have time, Kya!'

'You do, Mum, you work part time!'

'Yes, and I've got the housework to do, the shopping, and Lizzie...'

'That's no excuse. You don't go to your book club anymore, or the cinema with the girls. You used to love those evenings, even if he did track your every move. They were so important to you, and he used to dismiss them, the way he teased you about your *silly crafting club* and so you stopped going. Have you noticed they've stopped calling now?'

'We're grown-ups, everyone's busy with their own lives.' She's trying to convince herself.

'No, Mum, you've pushed them away and they've stopped trying. It's like all you want is to be around him, even though he treats you like a housekeeper.'

'He does not,' she says strongly.

'And the outbursts, over minor things? You say you're going to do something like take his suit to the dry cleaners or sort the spare room out, and you don't get around to it, so then you have to put up with a red-faced tirade about how uncooperative or useless you are? He loses his temper, but you defend him? In fact, you pander to him? It's pathetic.' I'm trying hard not to be too nasty. She's silent. No comeback. Again, I see the bitter indignation on her face, but in her eyes it's not him who's treating her unfairly, it's me. I hate hurting her, I hate to remind her what he's done to her, what he's taken away from her, but the only thing I can do is try and make her see sense. The truth hurts though, and sometimes no matter how hard you try, people just don't want to see it.

'And you always defend him! It's like you're addicted to him or something. You can't see how he controls you.'

'You're being ridiculous now.'

'No I'm not, Mum, you're acting blind. You can't see it, because he's clever. Men like him are. Clever and manipulative, and you can't see it. It's psychological abuse, and it's insidious, happening so gradually over the years you can't see it. But I can! And then something happens like the time he pushed you against the counter…'

'That was a one off, Kya.'

I ignore her and carry on, 'Like the time he pushed you against the counter and you couldn't walk for a week because of your bruised ribs, and instead of hating him or leaving him, you went entirely the other way, like you were trying to win back his affection. It's like the worse he gets, the more you want to please him? It's like Stockholm Syndrome or something.'

'Absurd!' she scoffs, and gets up from the table.

'It's not, it's called trauma bonding, you should look it up.'

'You're making this about me,' she says, taking food out of the fridge. Distract. Deflect. Deny.

'Well, it's never about me, is it?' I retort. 'Because I don't matter, do I? You're never going to put me first?'

'You're being silly, Kya.'

'Oh yes, of course I am. I'm just being silly. Silly Kya. Silly and ridiculous.' I've stopped trying to be calm and kind now, what's the point, the consideration is not reciprocated. I can't wait to get the hell out of here and leave them all behind for good.

## Lizzie

Mummy and Kya are shouting in the kitchen. I can hear Mummy saying she *tagonises* him and makes things worse. I hear them shouting and I just want to watch Frankie and Fuzzy so I turn up the volume. I hear the kitchen door slam and it makes me jump, then I can hear Kya running up the stairs and then her bedroom door slams really loud too. I can smell her sticks burning.

## Kya

I walk out of the kitchen and slam the door as hard as I
can. I go upstairs to my room and slam my bedroom door
too. I wouldn't dare do that if he was in, obviously, but he's
not, and I'm incensed, the frustration coursing through my
veins and threatening to burst them open. I'm wounded,
rejected, hurt. The feeling of abandonment from my own
mother, the lack of protection, the lack of care or under-
standing of what this does to me. It should be her obligation
and it should come without question, surely? Yet her love for
him, or dependence on him, or whatever bizarre obsession she
has with him, clearly takes priority. She doesn't see him as her
equal, she sees him as an authority figure, a person of high
status who wields all the power and control, a person that
should be obeyed and respected. I wonder where these deeply
ingrained values and beliefs come from. He's her source of
financial support, and rocking the boat or daring to have a
voice would be far more dangerous in her eyes than the risks
of doing absolutely nothing. And if *I* dare to speak up, call
him out, well that's just inconvenient and stressful for her.
*Don't make things awkward, just keep on pretending everything's fine and*

*it'll all go away.* Never mind the psychological effects it has on me. She doesn't want to be disloyal to him, he saved her when she had nothing, having been abandoned and rejected by her first husband. Maybe she thinks that if she challenges him we'd lose everything. He's a well-respected man with social standing, no one would believe her over him. It would break up the family, bring shame on him, and he'd make sure she suffered because of it. He would always win. We'd lose our home, maybe he'd take Lizzie. I wonder if it's all of these things that stop her from acting protectively. I don't know, who knows what she's thinking, if she's thinking at all. I do wonder though, if in the dead of night, when all is black and silent, if her conscience wakes up and forces her to think about it. I put on my music full blast and try to drown out my reality.

## Zak

I've had a few girlfriends, or *special friends,* but none of them have ever had this effect on me. I know I was a bit of a Jack the Lad in my old life, but I still had feelings, and I never felt this way, not once. And it wasn't because of the weed, or because I was high, it's because none of those girls were Kya. I think the longest relationship lasted about six months, and mainly because it was convenient. No, that sounds awful. Comfortable is a better word. She was a lovely girl, but she never understood me, and there was nothing of her to really understand. We didn't connect. She thought she was getting a bad boy, because that's what I was, on the outside. I hid the real me. The me that loved philosophy and literature, poetry and music. I put on a mask and I traded in my reality for a role. It was ok, I mean, it was fun – we hung out with the other kids, smoked pot, had sex. Because that's what we were supposed to do, right? But it was never about love, or mean-ing, or intimacy. It was perfunctory, half-hearted, mechanical. We never even took all our clothes off. I would never take off my long sleeved top. *Is this it?* I thought. *Is this as good as it gets?* I never dreamed I'd find someone who I'd connect with on a soul level, like Kya. Someone so deep, so passionate, so clever, so philosophical, so profound. So goddamn sexy. I scroll through my music app and find Tortured Heart. I select the first song and lie back on my bed and let the words wash over me, something about becoming numb, a spirit sleeping somewhere cold, imploring someone to wake it up and save it from the nothing it's become. It's dark, morbid even, but I can totally picture Kya listening to this.

I flashback to the way she looked at me, for that split second when her barriers were down, the way her eyes said *I want you too, but I'm scared*. It's as if she's speaking to me through my speakers, asking me to find her broken soul and lead it back home. She needs me, and I know I can save her.

# Kya

I'm trying to concentrate on homework but it's futile. He's back from work and I can hear them arguing downstairs. I hear the back door slam, and he's gone out. Mum will blame me, but I don't even care. At least I can relax a bit now he's out, as much as I can anyway, knowing he'll come home at some point. I open Messenger.

*Angry_Teenager:*
Thank you for being my friend.

*Tall_Dark_Dangerous:*
I will always be your friend. As long as you need.

*Angry_Teenager:*
Will that be enough for you? I mean, do you genuinely want to be my friend?

*Tall_Dark_Dangerous:*
Depends what your definition of friend is?

*Angry_Teenager:*
Official definition of 'friend': *a person whom one knows and with whom one has a bond of mutual affection, typically exclusive of sexual or family relations.*

I regret sending it immediately. The truth is, I don't want our friendship to be *exclusive of sexual relations*, not indefinitely.

*Tall_Dark_Dangerous:*
That's a bit uninspiring.

*Angry_Teenager:*
Well how would you describe it?

*Tall_Dark_Dangerous:*
*A friend is someone who gives you total freedom to be yourself, and especially to feel, or not feel. Whatever you happen to be feeling at any moment is fine with them.* —Jim Morrison, in case you didn't guess.

*Angry_Teenager:*
That sounds like a perfect way to sum it up. I like that version.

*Tall_Dark_Dangerous:*
I thought you might. And there are no restrictions of course...

No restrictions? Is he referring to the sexual relations? He's flirting with me. My stomach flutters and I feel that incredible tingling feeling coursing through my body. I ignore his comment on purpose. I feel like doing something really rebellious, destructive, dangerous even. *Fuck you! Fuck the world!*

*Angry_Teenager:*
I wonder what Morrison's thoughts were on love? I mean, he

was a deeply disturbed man, a pretty mean drunk, aggressive towards life and women, yet he is a literary genius who wanted to be remembered for his written word. I'd love to know the real him.

*Tall_Dark_Dangerous:*
He was a mean drunk, and he practically challenged people to leave him, but really he was insecure, and he loved deeply. He had a lot going on. He had a tough upbringing and he had his issues, probably not helped by all the LSD he took. But aside from the mean drunk part he was a poet, writing about deep, dark Freudian secrets. He was a genius who used his loathsomeness in a very clever way. We all have good and bad in us. Light and dark. And his thoughts on love, in his own words: *That's what real love amounts to – letting a person be what he really is. Most people love you for who you pretend to be. To keep their love, you keep pretending – performing. You get to love your pretence. It's true, we're locked in an image, an act – and the sad thing is, people get so used to their image, they grow attached to their masks. They love their chains. They forget all about who they really are. And if you try to remind them, they hate you for it, they feel like you're trying to steal their most precious possession.*

*Angry_Teenager:*
I don't ever want to have to pretend.

*Tall_Dark_Dangerous:*
You should never have to.

*Angry_Teenager:*
Have you ever been in love?

*Tall_Dark_Dangerous:*

No, not before I met you. Now I'm starting to realise what it really feels like.

I feel a blend of elation, excitement, lust, even if that was a bit cheesy. Adrenaline starts pumping around my body and I want to do something totally out of character. I want to run, I want to throw caution to the wind, I want to stand on top of a hill and scream *fuck you*! I want to be reckless, unruly, defiant. I want to rebel. I want to see what it feels like to be the uncontrollable, wicked degenerate I'm made out to be.

*Angry_Teenager:*
Want to do something crazy?

*Tall_Dark_Dangerous:*
What like?

*Angry_Teenager:*
I don't know, I just want to do something crazy. And I'm not talking about your level of danger, i.e. eating a dodgy chicken breast or failing to use conditioner, I mean let's really throw caution to the wind. Do something risqué. Can you borrow your mum's car?

*Tall_Dark_Dangerous:*
Yes!?!

*Angry_Teenager:*
Pick me up on the corner in ten minutes.

## Zak

S he's already there, waiting on the corner, dressed all in black, rucksack thrown over her shoulder. I pull over and as she gets into the passenger seat, I notice she looks different. She has a look about her, a look like she's either going to murder someone or jump on me and rip my clothes off right here and now. She looks ravishing.

'Are you ok?' I ask her.

'Just drive.' She looks ahead, fixedly.

'So, where are we going?'

'Just drive, I'll direct you.'

'Should I be scared?' I laugh. Of course, I'm not scared, but there's something about her tonight that tells me she's about to let shit go.

'*Are* you scared?' she asks, almost goading me.

'With you? Never.'

I reach over and squeeze her hand for a second, and glance at her briefly, as if to reassure her *I'd walk to the ends of the earth for you.* She half smiles back at me as if to return the compliment. There's a dangerous twinkle in her eye.

'Can you pull in here?'

I pull into the service station and she tells me to wait. I watch her run across the forecourt with her backpack slung over her shoulder. It's dark outside, but the bright lights shine down on the shape of her, a figure all in black, lithe and agile. I wonder what she could be getting in there and the thought that she might be planning on running away crosses my mind. She gets back in the car, slightly out of breath, emerald eyes twinkling.

'You done?'

'Done.'

We pull out and head onto the big stretch of road heading up to Mansell Mount.

'Drive faster,' she commands, then reaches forward and turns the music up loud.

I do as she says and accelerate. I glance over at her and she has her head flung back, eyes closed. She starts to sing along to the song on the radio, eyes still closed. I steal a look at her. I never thought someone could look angry and beautiful at the same time. She belts out the words now, something about cruel wanting, sinful love, wicked dreams. The song finishes and she looks at me and it's like a weight has lifted.

'Better?' I smile at her.

'Not yet, but I will be soon,' she smiles back.

We park up at Mansell Mount. It's deserted up here, and it feels like we are the last people on earth. I take out blankets from the boot and lay them down on the grass and sit down. I'm careful to respect her space, but she shuffles over to me. She reaches for her backpack and pulls out a packet of cigarettes, a box of matches and a bottle of vodka. I'm shocked.

'I didn't know you smoked?'

'I don't.' She's angrily trying to rip the cellophane off the packet. I realise that's what the service station stop was for.

'So why have you got cigarettes? And vodka?'

'Because I'm fucking sick of working so hard and doing

my best and still being treated like shit. Screw it all! I'm sick of being fucking sensible and goody-goody and boring. I'm going to do whatever the hell I want now. I'm sick of people controlling me.'

'You could never be boring,' I tell her.

She's still struggling with the cellophane.

'Well I am. I don't do anything. My wings are clipped. I'm trapped. Trapped in that fucking house with no voice, no power, and I study because it's my only way out but it's taking too fucking long and I cover my pain with *I'm fine* and I stay strong and I keep fighting but it's fucking breaking me and I want to break free and I want to cry and scream *fuck you all!* Scream and let it all out because it's fucking killing me inside and I'm going to explode!'

She barely comes up for breath and looks like she might actually explode. I take the cigarettes out of her hand and toss them to one side.

'They're not the answer, and you're better than that.'

'I just want to fucking scream!'

'Do it! Cry, yell, scream, do whatever you need to do to let it all out, and I'll be right here by your side. Just don't hold it in any longer because whatever it is, Kya, it's tearing you apart.'

She stands up, picks up a rock and screams as she throws it with such force. I stand up and go to her, pick up a huge rock and hand it to her.

'I fucking hate him!' she screams as she hurls this one into the distance.

'That's good, get it all out.'

'Fucking bastard!'

I'm ready with another rock, I pass it to her and she throws it.

'You don't fucking own me!'

I pass her another one.

'I wish you were fucking dead!'

By now she's crying. Hard, angry, bitter tears.

'You will *not* break me!' and with that last throw she stumbles back and I catch her and I feel her shaking, crying, the rage still alive despite her exhaustion from hurling rocks. I lead her back to the blanket and hold onto her as we sit down.

'Cry as hard as you want to. Get it all out. I'm here.'

She buries her face in my chest and she cries and cries, her sobs saying what her lips can't, whatever it is she's been holding on to for way too long. Soon the tears are no longer anger, they are sorrow and sadness, and eventually they die out too. Then there is silence and she lets her full weight fall onto me, lets me hold her, and her eyes have been closed the whole time. And now she tilts her face towards me and slowly, slowly, opens her eyes. She takes a deep breath in, then exhales loudly.

'Better?'

'Much better.' She disentangles herself from me.

'I'm sorry,' she says, pulling herself together and wiping her face with both hands.

'Never, ever apologise,' I tell her. 'You know, that which does not kill us makes us stronger,' I add, smiling.

'Nietzsche?'

'Of course.'

Now she smiles. There's no more anger or rage. Just a sea of calm.

'Are you ready to talk now?'

She doesn't answer.

'Kya, whatever it is you're dealing with you could probably do with talking about it. You've got to get it out.'

'I just did.'

'I don't mean that. You've got to talk, properly. You've obviously got some serious shit going on and you can't let it eat you up like this.'

She doesn't look at me, just hugs her knees to her chest. There's a slight chill in the air.

'You can trust me, Kya. I might be able to help. Whatever it is, you can trust me.'

She looks at me. She takes a deep breath in, and starts to talk.

## Kya

I've cried so much I feel like my own bones can no longer hold me up. And he held me through it all. I feel purged, spent.

'Are you ready to talk now?' he asks.

I know I can't put him through all that and not explain my psychotic outburst. What the hell. He probably thinks I'm a lunatic now anyway. I summon the courage to expose myself even more than I already have done, I take a deep breath and I tell him everything. He listens with empathy and doesn't interrupt, he just takes it in, as I lay myself completely bare. I've known him a week but he now knows more about me than anyone else in the entire universe.

When I finish speaking, he says, 'I can't promise to fix it, but I do promise that from now on you won't have to face it alone.'

I smile. 'Lie down with me?' I ask.

He smiles in agreement and we lie down together on our backs, our arms touching. He pulls a spare blanket over us. We lie in silence for a while and just stare up at the stars.

'Ever wonder what's out there?' I say eventually.

'All the time,' he replies. 'There's something incredible out there, just waiting, yet to be known.'

'Do you think there's life out there?' I'm feeling more philosophical than usual, if that's possible.

'Two possibilities – either we're alone in the universe or we're not.'

'Which one do you believe?'

'I think there's life out there, for sure. You know what Stephen Hawking said, don't you? *The idea that we are alone in the universe seems to be completely implausible and arrogant, considering the number of planets and stars that we know exist, it's extremely unlikely that we are the only form of evolved life.*

I nod, taking it all in. 'It's mind-boggling. I mean, it's so vast. And here we are, just small-time dreamers in an endless universe,' I say.

'We're part of it. The universe I mean. It's not a case of *us* and *it*, we are all part of *the whole*, and we call *the whole* the universe. We're inextricably linked. I believe the universe is on our side. We just have to believe, and respect it.'

He has such a way with words. His voice is deep, but soft, poetic. There's a real strength underneath his tranquility. I smile, and nudge myself closer to him. I reach out and take his hand in mine and despite how cold the night air has become, his hand is warm. I'm starting to think he's right, in that the universe has conspired to bring us two together. If I admitted this out loud he'd grin that cheeky, sexy grin and say, *Told you, I'm always right!*

# Zak

---

I could lie like this forever. It's like we are the only people on earth and the world is spinning just for us. She takes my hand, softly, and I have never felt so connected to anyone on a soul level. I silently thank the stars for answering my prayers.

'Does it scare you off, that I have demons?' she asks.

'Nothing you could ever do would scare me off,' I say. 'Anyway, we've all got monsters and demons inside us.'

She doesn't know how close to the truth this is, the extent of my demons.

'I feel like mine might take me over,' she says.

'How?'

'I sometimes imagine what it would be like to kill him. I mean, I wouldn't kill him obviously, but I imagine driving a knife into his chest. The demons inside me feel real, and I'm frightened one day they will win. You know what Nietzsche said about *Whoever fights monsters should see to it that in the process he does not become a monster himself?* Well, it's getting harder every day.'

'You are not a monster, and you will never be one. And you are stronger than your demons,' I tell her.

'You think so?' she asks, hopeful.

'I know so. When you face your demons, you become stronger than them. Only when you face them do they stop having power over you.'

'You sound like a person who knows a lot about demons?' She rests up on her elbow and looks at me, her face inches away from mine. She's quizzical. I know for sure that one day soon she's going to find out. But not now. Not tonight. Tonight is about her demons.

'Like I said, we all have them. Maybe one day I'll introduce you to mine. Maybe they'll get on great with yours, fall in love, and then leave us alone.'

She laughs, and lays her head down on my chest. I can smell incense in her hair, and I reach out and stroke it. It feels even better than I imagined. Soft, silky. I think in the end we are all searching for someone whose demons play well with our own.

## Kya

The kitchen lights are on and I know they're up, waiting for me. It's 2am and I have over a dozen missed calls and messages on my phone. I let myself in the back door and there they are, at the kitchen table. He stands up but Mum tells him to sit down, and miraculously, he does.

'Where the hell have you been?' She comes over to me and cups my face in her hands and checks me over. I must look like a mess from all the crying. I can't tell if she's going to burst into tears or yell at me.

'We were so worried!'

'Really? You don't seem overly concerned about me most of the time, so why start caring now?' I am calm, impassive.

'Where were you?'

'Out.'

Now he stands up.

'Your mother asked where you were, so answer her. Do you know what you've put us through?'

I don't even look at him, he is not deserving of my acknowledgement. I know this will wind him up.

'Leave it, I'll handle this,' Mum says, and I'm mildly impressed. Only mildly though.

'I should've text to let you know I was ok, Mum. I'm sorry for that.' My voice is quiet and dispassionate, emotionless. Because that's how I feel when I am around them now. Apathetic. 'And now, I'm going to bed.'

I sense his annoyance without looking at him, it must be taking all his strength not to explode into a fiery rage. *Try it,* I think. I walk past him without even glancing his way, like he's invisible. I feel a slight victory, smug, strong. *Fuck you,* I think. You don't get to hurt me anymore.

## Zak

I sneak in and creep up to my room. I lie on my bed, but despite how tired I am my eyes are wide open. I am totally bowled over by her. More addicted to her than I ever thought possible. I was never going to fall for a plain girl with no attitude, no demons, no grit. I love the dark side of her. I love how imperfectly perfect she is. Everyone, everything, has a dark side, even the moon, and I'm drawn to her more for it. You can't experience the beauty in life if you haven't seen the dark side, and there's good and bad, light and dark, in all of us. I should know.

## Kya

I close my bedroom door. Zak's words reverberate around my head, *'We all lose ourselves, and that's ok, just make sure your comeback is stronger than your setback. You can't let it change you, or it'll win.'* I smile. I feel strong again. I won't let anyone beat me down.

I fall asleep thinking of how it felt to be held by Zak. Safe and warm in his arms. Before long, I'm dreaming, and it's the hummingbird again. It's tap tap tapping against my bedroom window with its long, sharp beak. I wake up. *Am I dreaming?* I get out of bed gingerly and go over to my window. I draw the curtains back but there's nothing there. I get back into bed and fall back to sleep immediately, but then it starts again, *tap tap tap* on the window. I wake up again, or at least I think I'm awake, and go over the window and draw the curtains back, and there it is, its blue and green and purple hues shimmering in the moonlight. *Am I still dreaming?* It's desperate to get in, squawking loudly, anguish and despair in its tiny black eyes. What is it afraid of? I can feel its fear, but I can't move, once again I'm powerless to help. Then it stops squawking and is still, paralysed with fear. It stares at me for a second then *bang!*

it explodes and there's fragments of hummingbird splattered all over the glass. I jump, horrified, but I too am now paralysed with fear, and all I can do is stand and watch, as one last multicoloured feather floats slowly, slowly down.

I wake up tired and slightly confused by last night's dream. I have an uneasy feeling that perhaps it signifies my hardship isn't over, and that I'm not actually in control, but I brush it off. I don't want anything to interfere with my new-found strength. *Bring it on*, I think. *I don't care what you throw at me.* I go downstairs and they're all sitting there. They don't shout, he just tells me I'm grounded for a week. I shrug, unfazed. *Give me whatever you got, I can take it, because I'm stronger than I've ever been and you won't break me. Wanna ground me? So ground me. But ultimately you don't own me. One day soon I'll be out of here and you'll never ever be able to tell me what to do again. Shout at me? Go ahead, yell, but you won't scare me, you're just showing your own weakness and insecurity. Wanna hit me? Go on then. You might bruise my skin but you'll never break my soul.* And as I apply my thick, black eyeliner, I feel like no one can break me. I will rise from the fucking ashes.

## Lizzie

No one is talking at the breakfast table. I wonder why Mummy isn't at work still. Daddy says Kya is grounded for a week.

'What's grounded?' I ask.

'It's a consequence given to insolent teenagers when they violate a basic family rule, like a curfew.'

He is trying not to use his angry voice, but I can tell he's cross because it's more of an angry whisper and his eyes look mad.

Mummy tells him to stop it. I've never heard her talk like that to Daddy. I think she's cross with him.

The sicky feeling comes back in my tummy.

# Zak

I love my room. I've got the whole attic to myself, one large space, just for me. I've got an ensuite bathroom, a kettle, a small fridge. I've got everything I need. Mum respects my privacy and never comes up here. She's cool like that. I'm sitting at my desk trying to study but I'm going crazy, thinking about Kya. I sit back and stare at my red wall, wonder what she's doing. I guess she'll be studying too. I open up messenger.

*Tall_Dark_Dangerous:*
I'm going crazy not being able to see you.

*Angry_Teenager:*
You saw me three hours ago. Are you going soft on me?

*Tall_Dark_Dangerous:*
Walking to school and back is not enough. I wish you were here now. I want to get to know you more.

*Angry_Teenager:*

Aren't you meant to be studying?

*Tall_Dark_Dangerous:*
Yes, but I can't concentrate.

*Angry_Teenager:*
Ok, what do you want to know? Ask me anything.

*Tall_Dark_Dangerous:*
Ok, favourite ice cream?

*Angry_Teenager:*
Cookie dough. Yours?

*Tall_Dark_Dangerous:*
Chocolate. Favourite movie?

*Angry_Teenager:*
The Theory of Everything. Yours? Please don't say Star Wars.

*Tall_Dark_Dangerous:*
Eternal Sunshine of the Spotless Mind. Favourite food? PS
Star Wars? I'm offended.

*Angry_Teenager:*
Chinese food. Yours? And for the record, I knew you wouldn't
be a Star Wars fan.

*Tall_Dark_Dangerous:*
Same. Chinese food! See? Meant to be together. I'm always
right! Who would you have at your house for a dinner party,
dead or alive?

*Angry_Teenager:*

Mary Wollstonecraft. Virginia Woolf. Maybe Charles Melton. You? Let me guess, Jim Morrison? Nietzsche? Who else?

*Tall_Dark_Dangerous:*
Jim Morrison and my dad. And you. I'd want you there. PS Charles Melton, the South Korean heartthrob? We need to talk about this… ;-) Next question. What do you want to be? I.e. what job?

*Angry_Teenager:*
I'm still trying to figure out what type of job I'd get with an English Language and Literature degree? Maybe something in research, publishing, academia. How about you? What will you do when you've got your first class Philosophy degree?

*Tall_Dark_Dangerous:*
I don't know. Probably something humanitarian. Maybe even go into psychotherapy. Something where I'm giving back, helping people. Ok, worst and favourite part of your body?

*Angry_Teenager:*
I am not answering that!

*Tall_Dark_Dangerous:*
Chicken. Ok, what are you most afraid of?

*Angry_Teenager:*
Not getting into university! Unfulfilled potential. Lizzie growing up with him as a dad. You?

*Tall_Dark_Dangerous:*
Losing you.

*Angry_Teenager:*

Do you have any hideous secrets or psychotic tendencies that I should know about?

*Tall_Dark_Dangerous:*
I definitely don't have psychotic tendencies...

*Angry_Teenager:*
Then we should be good :-)

*Hideous secrets.* If she were here, perhaps my face would give it away.

# Kya

It's been three days and thankfully he hasn't said a word to me. I don't know what Mum has done to make him keep out of it, but he's stayed out of my way as much as I've stayed out of his. But I know the pattern, it won't go on like this indefinitely. He's like a ticking time bomb, bound to go off at any second. It's predictable, unavoidable. Mum is on shift tonight and I'm starting to feel tense already, so I light an incense stick and breathe deeply as the smell of Nag Champa wafts round my room, calming me. Me and Zak are getting by on constant messaging, and I find it surprising how well you can get to know someone via black and white words on a screen.

I open my laptop and log on.

*Angry_Teenager:*
What are you up to?

*Tall_Dark_Dangerous:*
Doing what I always do when I'm not with you.

*Angry_Teenager:*
What's that?

*Tall_Dark_Dangerous:*
Thinking about you.

*Angry_Teenager:*
Anything in particular?

*Tall_Dark_Dangerous:*
Yes. Something very particular.

*Angry_Teenager:*
I'm intrigued?

*Tall_Dark_Dangerous:*
Do you have any fantasies?

I stiffen up. How can I tell him I've never been with anyone? I know I want him to be the one. I buy some time.

*Angry_Teenager:*
Fantasies?

*Tall_Dark_Dangerous:*
Yeh, like you and me, alone in the bedroom together kind of fantasies.

*Angry_Teenager:*
……………..?

I've memorised every part of him, his shiny black hair, his dark eyes, his angular features, the look of his soft lips, his hands, big, protective, soft. Him towering above me, his broad shoulders, how I felt his muscular chest underneath his black top when I lay my head on him at Mansell Mount. Now I can't stop thinking about what it might look like under that top. I think about him holding me tight and kissing me, his big arms around me. But for some reason I'm nervous to type this.

*Tall_Dark_Dangerous:*
I'll start. I spend a large proportion of my day imagining what it will be like when I kiss you for the first time.

*Angry_Teenager:*
Presumptuous! How do you know that's going to even happen?

*Tall_Dark_Dangerous:*
Don't be coy, you know it's going to happen.

*Angry_Teenager:*
OK, I'm thinking about that too.

*Tall_Dark_Dangerous:*
I want to hold your face gently in mine, look into your beautiful eyes, then kiss you slowly and gently.

*Angry_Teenager:*
And then?

*Tall_Dark_Dangerous:*
You'd kiss me back, softly at first, but then more urgently, pulling me closer to you.

I imagine my hands running over his chest now, putting my hands up his t-shirt and feeling his firmness, grabbing the belt of his jeans and pulling him closer to me.

*Angry_Teenager:*
Go on…

*Tall_Dark_Dangerous:*
I want to run my hands through your hair. I want to kiss your neck, softly and gently at first…

I touch my neck, imagining him kissing me there, and my skin tingles in anticipation.

*Tall_Dark_Dangerous:*
I want to know every part of you. I want to kiss every part of you.

I don't want him to stop.

*Angry_Teenager:*
And?

*Tall_Dark_Dangerous:*
I'd undress you slowly. So slowly. Taking in every part of you, stopping every moment to kiss you…

*Angry_Teenager:*
Keep going…

*Tall_Dark_Dangerous:*
I'd take your hand and lead you over to the bed…

*Angry_Teenager:*
And then??????

*Tall_Dark_Dangerous:*
And then… You'll have to wait and see :-)

## Zak

For some reason, despite how tired I am, I can't drift off to sleep. Thoughts of Kya, thoughts of kissing her neck. I wonder if she's thinking of me now. Eventually I drift off, and I dream. I'm lying on my bed and she walks into my room, closes the door behind her. I make as if to get up but she points at me, silently ordering me to stay where I am. She walks over to me, a sultry look on her face. She's dressed all in black, tight black jeans, long sleeved tight black top, long black boots. Her hair is blacker than ever, her lips redder than blood, and her eyes have emerald fire in them. I sit up, but she pushes me back down on the bed roughly, then straddles me. I go to speak but she puts her finger to my lips, it's clear she's in control. She leans down and kisses me. I kiss her back, and she bites my lip, a little too hard, then she moves onto my neck, alternating between sensual kisses and biting. *Sit up!* I do as I'm told and she pulls my t-shirt urgently over my head, then pushes me back down again. She's kissing my neck again, moving down to my chest. Her kisses feel like hot lava on my stomach and I'm nervous but excited. The anticipation burns inside me as she kisses all the way down to where my jeans are, and I'm thinking *please don't stop*, but then she moves slowly back up my stomach, kissing all the way, and as she does so, she speaks the words so softly I barely hear them. *I know your big secret.* Then she stops kissing me, straightens up, and stares into my eyes. *It's your fault he's dead.*

## Lizzie

I don't like it this morning, Daddy is angry.

'There are going to be new rules around here. This is my house, and people are going to learn to respect me.'

I think he is talking to himself. He is making my breakfast and he puts my bowl down so hard on the table it makes me jump.

'Do I aspect you Daddy?'

'Of course you do, angel, you're perfect.' He kisses my head. 'But Kya needs to buck her ideas up and remember who this house belongs to. Now, angel, which cereal would you like?'

Kya used to make my breakfast when Mummy was at work, but now she stays in her room and doesn't come out until just before I go. I feel a bit sick in my tummy but I try to eat my hoops. Now Daddy is saying something about Kya's loud music and that she is going to learn. I wish she would stop making him mad and just be a good girl and then he wouldn't get so cross with her. I don't want him to be cross with her. I can hear her music upstairs but she'll be downstairs soon. She always comes to say goodbye to me before Katy comes to get me.

## Kya

I can't wait to see him this morning. Right now I feel like a normal girl, getting ready for school in my bedroom, doing my hair and makeup, feeling excited about meeting my boyfriend. Is he my boyfriend? I turn my music up slightly louder than usual, feeling the adrenaline rush through my veins, but when I go downstairs the air is thick with hostility, resentment brimming in the atmosphere. I tell myself to stay calm, stay strong, it will be fine. Lizzie runs over to me and throws her arms around my legs.

'Kya!'

'Morning, goldilocks! How's my baby girl?'

I kiss the top of her head and when she looks up, she looks worried. It's then I hear things slamming around in the kitchen.

'Daddy is cross this morning,' she whispers.

Ticking time bomb.

'Has he been cross with you, sweetie?'

'No. He said there are going to be new rules in the house and you are going to learn to aspect him.'

I am nervous and annoyed at the same time. Lizzie

shouldn't have to be exposed to this. She shouldn't have to witness his rage, or his hatred of me. It's not a healthy environment for her, and it's only going to get worse for her as she gets older. And what about when I'm gone?

'Don't you worry, sweetie,' I try and convince her, 'I'm a big girl and I can look after myself. You just keep being a super girl at school, and don't ever let anyone dull your shine, ok?'

'What does dull my shine mean?'

'It means, keep being a bright sparkly star!' I smile, feigning cheeriness for her sake, but there's no denying the panicky feeling in the pit of my stomach.

It's not knowing what to expect that's the worst thing. It's a daily question, *What is he going to do today? What landmines am I going to have to avoid?* I have a ball of anxiety in my stomach. The guessing. Will he blank me, refuse to look at me or speak to me? I hope so. Will he make a few cutting comments about my look or my attitude or my general existence? I can handle that. Will he shout and scream and rant like a madman until he's purple in the face and spitting everywhere? Or will this be one of the times where shouting is not enough? It's the not knowing. It's the walking on eggshells, the inevitability that they're going to crack.

# Zak

I'm still tired after last night's crazy dream. It was so real, and still so raw when I woke up, but it's fading now. I still have the dreams, but less so now. They're slightly different each time, but each one has the same message – *It's your fault he's dead!* Sometimes it's even more cruel, *You killed him!* I use the techniques my old psychotherapist showed me to push the thoughts away, turning them towards Kya instead. I'm heading towards the graveyard and our usual meeting spot but I'm so lost in thoughts of her that I find myself walking down her street and towards her house. I've never actually been to her house. I've always got the feeling she doesn't want me to as she always insists we meet at the gates, but she's never actually said *don't come to my house.* I knock on the door and wait. A man answers. *That's him. That's the bastard she's told me all about.* I'm momentarily shocked as he looks like a normal man. I'm not sure what I was expecting. Perhaps I expected him to look like, I don't know, a bully, a tyrant? What does a bully even look like? I'm sure I recognise his face though.

'Yes?' he says, rather curtly.

'Hi,' I say, confident yet respectful. 'I'm here for Kya?' I look him directly in the eyes. He glares at me. He's tall, with gingery hair and a matching moustache. Where do I recognise him from? He looks me up and down silently for what feels like an inordinate amount of time.

'Kya, someone is here for you,' he snaps, then closes the door most of the way. I'm not being invited in then.

'You're not going anywhere yet, you haven't eaten breakfast or cleaned your shoes,' he says, behind the semi-closed door.

Kya comes to the door looking extremely anxious.

'You shouldn't come here,' she says, clearly uncomfortable. 'Go ahead, I'll see you at the gates in a minute.'

God, I hope I haven't made things worse for her. I don't like the look of that guy at all.

## Kya

Lizzie was right, he's angry. He hasn't said anything yet but it's brewing. He's like a walking volcano, likely to erupt any minute, hot lava spewing from his stupid head. I remember learning about volcanoes in geography. Most volcanoes give warning signs weeks or months before they erupt. Signs like tiny earthquakes beneath the volcano, or in his case, passive aggressive behaviour, cutting remarks, criticisms, taunting, goading. Then comes the slight inflation, or swelling of the volcano, the increased emissions of heat and gas from the vents (visible anger, change in atmosphere, makes everyone in the house uncomfortable, his fury lurking beneath the surface, getting ready to blow). In some cases, things progress much quicker. There may be noticeable steaming or fumarolic activity, new or enlarged areas of hot ground (slamming down of objects, cussing, letting everyone know he's angry). These are caused by magma pushing upward through the rock under the volcano (his face takes on a molten shade of red). The ground will eventually crack open to allow the steam to escape, known as a hydrothermal or phreatic eruption. I've learned to read the warning signs.

Unfortunately, there is no way to stop a volcano erupting, you can only watch and wait, and unless you have somewhere to hide, it's inevitable you will fall victim to the fiery fit. I have nowhere to hide, and I cannot flee. So it becomes about acceptance and readiness. You learn to closely watch its every move, understand when it might burst to life. You know when you're safe, understand where you can safely tread, where you need to steer clear. You know the exclusion zones. And most importantly, you always, always know your evacuation routes.

I don't want to be here a second longer than I have to this morning so I grab some fruit, fill up my water bottle and prepare to leave. Lizzie's already been picked up so I'm surprised when the doorbell goes. I hear Zak's voice and I freeze. *What is he doing here?*

'Hi, I'm here for Kya.' His tone is confident yet respectful. If I had a normal life, a proper dad, I'd be proud to introduce him to my family. But I don't have a normal life. Or a proper dad. Or any dad.

'Kya, someone is here for you.' His tone is ice cold. Menacing. He closes the door most of the way on Zak, sending a clear message. I want to shrivel up and die.

'You're not going anywhere until you've eaten breakfast and cleaned your shoes.'

The volcano is about to erupt. I tell Zak to go ahead and wait for me at the gates. I'm ready to leave now but I need him out of the way quickly to avoid any humiliating scenarios. I close the door and go and grab my things from the kitchen.

I head back towards the front door but *he's* standing there, hands on his hips, blocking my evacuation route. I can see the magma pushing up through his body, the red hue underneath his pockmarked skin. I can feel the slight tremors, see him shaking with anger, the steam desperate to escape.

'Excuse me,' I say, not looking at him, my voice trying to

strike a balance between not showing my nerves and not coming across as cocky or antagonistic. It's exhausting.

'You're not going anywhere until you've had breakfast.'

'I can't eat breakfast, I'm not hungry this early in the morning.' How many times do I have to tell him this? 'Anyway, I've got fruit.'

'You are going to eat breakfast and you are going to clean your shoes!' He's shouting now. I feel the anger and frustration rise inside me, my own river of lava flowing angrily, threatening to spill over.

'Why do you have to be like this? You don't get to control me!' I try not to shout but the anger has a life of its own.

'This is MY house and therefore, yes, I DO get to set the rules. And whilst you're living under my roof you will obey me!'

'*Obey* you?' I shout, unable to keep the loathing from my voice. I've stopped trying to stay calm. I stare at him, incredulous. My heart is pounding in my chest, adrenaline pumping, rage mixed with fear, the knot in my stomach, the invisible fist clenching my heart, the lump in my throat, the hot, angry yet fearful tears poking the back of my eyeballs, the mixture of emotions. I want to scream and strike out and hit him with a heavy object and hit him and hit him and hit him until he lies on the floor dead and bleeding. *Know your evacuation route*. My eyes are on the door, but he's still standing in front of it.

'I'm going to be late.' I try and step around him but he sidesteps and blocks the way.

'You can't stop me from leaving the house!' I push past him and reach for the handle. I manage to pull the door open but he's got hold of my jacket and he's pulling me. The door is ajar and if I lose this opportunity to get out of the house I'm done for.

'You are going to learn some respect and you ARE going to do as you're told!' he yells.

The pressure inside me is building. My own magma, my own molten rage. My body is used to the physical effects of anger, triggering my body's fight or flight response. My foot is in the door and I squirm through it and break free.

'FUCK YOU!' I scream as loud as I can, the words escaping violently from my mouth. At that precise moment I feel a rush of exhilaration from daring to stand up to him, but feel equally terrified at the consequences I know will follow.

# Zak

Something stops me from going on ahead, and I loiter at the end of her street, my eyes not leaving her door. A few minutes pass. I have a sense of foreboding. Another few minutes. Then the door flies open and she bursts out.

'FUCK YOU!'

I hear her scream, and in a blur she's running down the path, and he's running after her. He's too quick. He's going to get her. Instinctively I run, my adrenal glands flooding my body with adrenaline and cortisol, ready to fight. *I'm going to kill him.* My brain shunts the blood away from my gut and towards my muscles in preparation for impending physical exertion. I sprint down the road, watching as he grabs her jacket and tries dragging her back towards the house. She's screaming at him to get off her as he pins her up against the wall by her throat. And then I'm there. I drag him off her and slam him as hard as I can into the wall, knocking the breath out of him. He's tall but I'm taller still, and I tower over him. He's shocked, his eyes like a rabbit in headlights. *Pathetic bully.* I hold him against the wall, and we stare each other out.

'Let. Go. Of. Me,' he hisses, his breath squeaking as I squeeze my hands tighter around his throat.

'No! Not until you promise you will never lay a finger on her again.' I turn to Kya who is standing stock still, staring at me with a look of utter shock and disbelief.

'Do you know who I am, young man?' His eyes are burning with rage but his voice is weak and raspy.

'I don't give a damn who you are, you don't get to touch her! Do you understand me?'

He is silent, unaccustomed to anyone wielding power over him.

I slam him back against the wall again. 'I SAID, do you understand me?'

'Understood,' he spits pathetically, his voice restricted as he vigorously struggles for air. Blood vessels bulge visibly in his cheeks and I want to squeeze harder still. I wonder how long it would take for him to lose consciousness – one minute too long and he could die. I let go of him and the blood drains from his face. He gasps for air, not taking his eyes off me, glaring with fear and loathing in his eyes. I hold his stare, the adrenaline still coursing around my body. I stand my ground, staring him down, slightly nervous that he might hit me, but half hoping he will. *Bring it on, see what you'll get,* I think.

He straightens his shirt collar, trying to regain some composure, and walks back to the house. He stops on the step, turns around and glares fiercely at Kya.

'I'll deal with you later.'

And with that he closes the door.

# Kya

'**A**re you ok?' His first thought is of me, as he protectively searches my face for marks or clues. 'You're shaking.'

He cups my face in his hands and looks into my eyes, as if trying to read me, and I don't think I could love anyone as much as I do him, right now, but I'm speechless, literally speechless. I think I'm in shock. I feel a certain elation at having watched *him* get put in his place like that, and I feel a rush of awe and gratitude for Zak, wolf-like and brave, risking himself to stick up for me. But I also feel the sting of humiliation, and the fear and sadness that it's not actually over. It won't ever be over until I've packed up and left for good. I feel hatred, dread, despair. I can't describe the torrent of emotions, all jumbled up. I feel like I might throw up.

'Let's get out of here,' Zak says, as he picks up my bag. He takes my hand and I let him lead me away towards the graveyard. Our graveyard. Once safely inside the large brick walls, we sit down on our bench and I burst out laughing. Zak looks at me, bemused.

'I thought you were going to kill him!' My laugh sounds worryingly sinister.

'I *wanted* to kill him!' he admits, though I know he doesn't mean it literally.

'No, I'm being serious. I actually thought for a moment that he might die. Like, properly die. Cease to live. Certifiably dead. Alive no more. I could see the panic on his face, his beady little eyes angry when he realised he wasn't the person with all the power. I thought his head was going to explode.' I'm laughing maniacally now. I can hear myself, like I'm outside my body, looking down, and even I'm worried about myself. Perhaps I've lost it, finally cracked, all this has sent me mental, unstable, unhinged, certainly disturbed.

'I think you're in shock, Kya. Here, drink some water.' Zak passes me a bottle of water and I stare at it. I've stopped laughing now.

'I actually wanted him to die.' My voice cracks, it's low, my eyes fixed on the water.

Zak has his arms around me. He rubs my back.

'What the hell am I going to do now?' I say, and the dread washes over me like a tsunami.

'We need to talk to someone, Kya. You can't live like this. He can't go on treating you like this. Is there anyone you can think of we can go talk to now? What time does your mum finish her shift?'

'I've told you, she won't do anything. She'll take his side as always, and I'll just be an inconvenience for putting her in the middle and causing her grief.'

'Then we need to talk to someone else. Have you got any relatives?'

'No.'

'A teacher then?'

I laugh, 'Absolutely no way. Nothing would happen. I don't have any bruises. What would I say? *Excuse me, Mr Wilson, my step dad calls me names and makes me eat breakfast and clean my shoes in the morning?* I'd get laughed out of his office.'

'No, Kya. You'd tell him, or whoever you decide to go to, *everything*, and I mean everything! It's abuse, Kya. He's a bully! You may not have bruises, but it's psychological, mental, emotional abuse. You have the right to feel safe in your own home. And there's no telling what he'll do next. You can't let him get away with that! Someone has to stop him.

'It won't work, Zak. He'll play the trusted, respected councillor, all prim in his posh suit, loved and admired by everyone in the community.'

'That's how I know his face, he's that councillor!' Zak says. 'Slimy fucking creep.'

'And then I'd be in even more trouble for causing trouble for him. It would make home life even worse. If that's possible.'

'He can't go on treating you like this, Kya, he just can't.'

I don't say anything, I just look at the ground, working out, again, how long it is until I can leave home for uni, as if it will have magically changed since the last time I thought about it. Two years, still. It's too long.

'What's he like with your mum, and Lizzie?'

'Lizzie, he adores. She can do no wrong. Which she can't, I mean, she's a five-year-old girl and she's perfect in every way. He treats her like royalty. I've never heard him shout at her, and I can't imagine he'd ever hit her, but who knows, when she's a teenager. Who knows what he'll be like then, perhaps he'll have even less self-control. Maybe he won't be able to help himself, he's clearly deranged, and I won't be around then to protect her, I'll be long gone. The thought of leaving her when I go to uni scares me so much. What if something happened to her? What if she ends up going through what I've been through?'

'You have to put yourself first, Kya. It's your mum's responsibility to look after Lizzie and ensure she's safe.'

I laugh, 'Yeh, and she was meant to do the same for me.

I'm her daughter too. She's meant to protect me, put me first, yet she doesn't.'

'That's got to hurt?' He looks at me sympathetically.

'That's the worst part of it. All those times I was being tormented, bullied, physically dragged around, even the time he punched me in the stomach. She could have protected me, and she chose not to, period.'

The barriers are up. I feel tears pricking the back of my eyeballs but I'm forcing them back. I stare at a stone on the ground, nudge it one way then the other with my boot.

'Maybe it's the best she can do? I mean, I'm not saying it's right, she *should* be putting you first and protecting you, but what if she feels powerless to do anything? Has he ever threatened her? Hit her?'

'He's thrown plates. Screamed and yelled. Left a fist mark in the wall once. Thrown a casserole over her. I remember it like it was yesterday, they were arguing in the kitchen. It was only a few years ago, Lizzie was just a baby. They argued over something trivial and he went into one of his frenzies. Mum had made a huge pot of casserole for dinner and it was on the side. He went for her. Just lunged for her, had hold of her jumper and they were sort of grappling with each other. She was in the corner and he was clearly overpowering her. I was screaming at him to get off her, but of course that didn't achieve anything. Then he picked up the casserole dish from the worktop and emptied it all over her head before storming out of the house and screeching off in his car.'

'Jesus Christ.' Zak shakes his head.

'The look on her face still breaks my heart now. The way he humiliated her. She stood there all covered in casserole. He could have scalded her, but luckily it had cooled. I knew how hurt she was. She loves him, for some stupid, twisted, reason, she fucking loves him.'

'So what happened then?'

'I begged her to leave him, again. But once she'd calmed down and the initial shock wore off, she was back to her usual self. She brushed it off and stuck up for him. She laughed it off and said things like *Don't be silly, it's not like he hit me!* Like it's normal behaviour for your husband to throw a massive pan of hot food over you. I felt so sorry for her, the way he'd upset her. She tried to hide it from me but we were so close back then, I knew. I could see the pain and humiliation in her eyes, but she smiled and brushed it off.'

Zak squeezes my shoulder. I'd forgotten his arm was around me.

'It was so confusing. I felt sorry for her, yet I resented her for not giving me the same consideration when he directed his temper towards me. I desperately wanted to protect her, for her to be safe, and happy, but then I'd think about how she wasn't giving that to me. Such conflicting feelings, love and hate. It drove a wedge between us. And every time he bullied me or humiliated me in front of friends and she'd stick up for him, it was just like another betrayal.'

'Maybe she feels trapped?'

'I think at first she was just so grateful that he'd *rescued* her. She was a single mum struggling to make ends meet, then this dashing man in a suit comes along with his good job and his nice house and his big estate car, promising to take care of her. Suddenly her life's easier. And over the years it may not have been perfect, but in her eyes, it's better than the alternative.'

'What's that?'

'Well if at any point she realised she was married to an abusive monster who treated her like shit and tormented her daughter, she'd have to be really brave to leave – she'd have to start over. She'd have to go back to housing help, get a full-time job to support us, and she'd still probably struggle. She'd have to be brave enough to leave him and go it alone. Which is what I'd do. But that's too hard for her. It's hard to stand up to a bully. It's easier to stay, brush the bad bits under the carpet, pretend they don't happen. And now, as the years go by, she won't even consider leaving, she's too reliant on him. But what I can't get my head around is the fact that she actually loves him. She genuinely loves him, even when he treats her like shit. Even though she has no friends left, no money of her own, no say. It's like she enjoys being in this position.'

'Maybe she feels like it's the best she'll get, or maybe like it's all she deserves? I'm not sure. What do I know? I just know it's not fair for you to have to go through this, Kya. It's one thing living with someone who shouts and has mood swings, but he's not safe. I've seen the guy, and I don't trust him. There's no telling what he might do. I don't think you're safe there.'

I feel sick. I know he's right. But what can I do, where can I go? 'I've got another two years to get through before I can leave.'

'You can't stay there.'

'What choice do I have?'

'We'll work it out. But for now, shall we go get a coffee? It's cold. You're shaking again.'

I look at my watch.

'Shit. I've missed registration.'

'That's the least of your worries. Fuck school today. Come on, let's throw caution to the wind. Do something daring. I bet you've never skived?'

'Ha ha, no I haven't, and I'm not about to start now! School's too important to me. It's my ticket out of here. Have you ever skived?'

'Nope, but I'm feeling daring, plus we've already missed registration,' he looks at me and raises an eyebrow. 'Come on, I dare you.'

I throw my hands up in surrender and grin at him. 'Ok,

but just so you can add it to your list of extremely dangerous and daring things.'

We laugh and walk off, his hand protectively around mine, leading me, me not caring where we're going, as long as I'm with him.

## Zak

I think it's pertinent to call these extenuating circumstances
*– a serious and exceptional factor outside of our control which has
adversely affected our ability to get to school today.* We walk, we hold
hands, we talk, we laugh, despite the circumstances of this
morning. We head out of the graveyard and find a cafe where
we drink hot chocolate and eat warm, buttery teacakes. We
head back to *our graveyard* as Kya refers to it. I like the sound
of *our*. We walk around and look at the gravestones, talk about
the people who are buried here, wonder who they were, what
they were like, what kind of lives they had, how they died. We
walk and talk all day. We still haven't kissed, but I know it's
coming, and when it does it will be worth waiting for. I know
that, once we do kiss, that's all I'll want to do when I'm with
her, so for now I want us to talk as much as possible, to get to
know everything I possibly can about her and how she thinks
and how she views the world. She smiles occasionally, and
when she does, I see the light break through her eyes, but the
dark cloud is there, always, hanging over her shoulders. I can't
pretend it's not there either. The reality is, she has to go home
at some point, and he will be there.

At the end of the day, we stand in the graveyard, at our gates, within the walls, *our* walls, and I don't want to say goodbye. I don't want her to go home, but she's adamant she's ok, and says her mum will be home so it won't be as bad. But I can see the worry darkening her face. I need to talk to her about something really important, so I rest my hand on her cheek and look her in the eyes, conveying how serious it is.

'Kya, if you're in danger, or he threatens you, you have to do everything you can to get out of there, ok?'

'I don't think he's a danger to my life or anything, just my sanity. I can handle it.' She tries to laugh it off, but I see her unease.

'I'm serious, Kya, I don't trust that guy. I think he's capable of anything, and he's not going to let what happened this morning go. Did you see how pissed he was that someone had overpowered him for a change?'

She knows just as well as I do that he's going to make her suffer for this morning.

'I need to show you something. If he attacks you, or overpowers you like he did this morning, you need to poke him in the eyeballs.'

She laughs. Man she looks beautiful when she laughs, but this is serious, I need her to stay safe. I carry on, to show her I mean what I'm saying.

'An eye poke can be really effective. Use your index and middle finger together like this, and poke, as hard as you can. No matter how big and strong someone is, no one can just shrug off an eye poke. His hands will automatically go to his face, giving you time to get away. And if you can't get to his eyes then you kick him in the balls as hard as you can, or you bite him or do whatever it takes to get him off you so you can get the hell out of that house, ok?'

She nods at me, and I can't quite believe we're having to have this conversation.

'Promise?' I cup her face in my hands and we stare into each other's eyes. Her eyes glance at my lips, and automatically my eyes dart to hers. Electricity runs through my body, but I remind myself that the anticipation of pleasure is pleasure itself. *Be patient. Enjoy this time.* I know she wants me to kiss her, but instead I kiss her on the cheek then wrap my arms around her, holding her tight. She holds me back, neither of us wanting to let go first, and I want to stay like this for eternity, just us, like one single soul that inhabits two bodies.

## Kya

As expected, his silver estate is not in the drive so I know he's not back from work. I usually enjoy this time of day, where I get Mum and Lizzie to myself for a couple of hours. I get the feeling I'm not going to enjoy it today, though. Despite the fact that I'm the innocent party in all of this, I know he will have done a good job of telling Mum his side of the story at lunchtime, and somehow, I will be implicated as the troublemaker. I go into the house with trepidation, and they're in the kitchen, Mum's preparing dinner, Lizzie's sitting at the table with her crayons.

'Hey,' I say, already exhausted by what's about to come.

'Kya! Look, I drawed this picture! It's us!'

'Hey, baby girl, let me see!'

I sit down next to her and look at her picture. I wonder why kids always draw the sun in the corner of the page. A big waxy yellow sun. I did the same. Me and Mum used to sit for hours, drawing, colouring, back when it was just us. Back when I was my mother's little girl. Back when she loved me more than anything or anybody. I felt so safe. I would draw our dream house. It was a big square, and the windows were always in the corners. It would have a chimney with smoke coming out of it, rising up to the fluffy white clouds and the upside-down v's that were meant to be birds. The room on the top right was always mine and the one on the left was Mum's. Mine always had pink curtains and Mum's were orange. The downstairs windows would usually have blue or purple curtains, and there would always be a vase of flowers in the window, pink or red. *Because you love flowers, don't you, Mummy?* I'd say. *Yes, darling*, she'd laugh, and stroke my hair, or kiss the top of my head. Sometimes I would draw a straight path, sometimes a wiggly one, and there would always be an apple tree, bright green with rosy red blobs coloured onto it. Sometimes there would be a little black cat on the grass, or a duck pond. *This is our dream house, Mummy, and one day we will live there, and I will pick you flowers every day*, I'd tell her, proudly showing off my picture. *I've got everything I need right here, my darling*, she'd reply. *As long as we have each other, that's all we'll ever need.* I feel a physical pain in my heart at the memory.

I look at Lizzie's drawing.

'This is Mummy,' she points to the picture. In it, Mum is smiling a huge pink smile.

'This is Daddy,' she points to him. He's holding Mum's hand and he's smiling. He has a bright orange moustache. In crayon they look like two normal people.

'This is me,' she has drawn herself holding a balloon, and she's wearing her favourite shiny red shoes from the TV. She's wearing a pink dress with a red love heart on the front.

'And this is you!' she beams, pointing at the picture.

I don't look right in the picture. Somehow I don't fit. Everyone is pretty in pink and smiling and holding hands, and there I am, standing on the sidelines, dressed head to toe in black. Black jeans, black boots, black long-sleeved t-shirt, black hair, black eyes. The only colour is the blood red of my lips.

'Wow, you did my hair really well!' I say, overenthusiastically.

Lizzie beams, 'I did your lipstick too!'

'It's perfect,' I say, kissing the top of her head. But I'm lying, because nothing's perfect. Not the picture, not the reality, none of it.

'So,' Mum says. 'Are you going to tell me what happened this morning?'

'I'm assuming he's already told you his version, so why don't you go first?'

'I'm asking you, Kya.' She tucks a tea towel into the waistband of her trousers and leans against the chair, looking at me with a look that says *Let's get this over with, I'll pretend I'm listening to you and seeing things from your point of view but really I just want this all to go away.*

'Ok, I'll tell you.' I stand tall, hands on hips, and look her square in the eyes. 'He attacked me!'

Mum's face says *I really don't need this right now.*

'First of all, he wouldn't let me leave the house. He physically blocked the doorway, Mum. What kind of sane adult does that?'

Mum's face says *Don't exaggerate.*

'So you told him to *F off?*'

And there it is. The blame. Of course it's my fault, I was being difficult, I swore at him.

'Yes,' I say, infuriated, 'because he wouldn't let me out of the house, Mum! And when I tried to get past him he physically grabbed me and tried to drag me back inside!'

'He said you refused to clean your shoes.'

'Yes!' I say in exasperation, 'because you don't polish Doc Martens, Mum, and I walk through the graveyard to school so it would be an utterly pointless exercise anyway.'

'You know he has standards, he just likes everyone to look smart and play the part.'

'Play the part? Have you heard yourself? Play what part, Mum? I don't want to play a part! I just want to be *me!* And I want to be *me* in a safe environment where I'm not tormented or forced to eat breakfast or polish my shoes against my will!'

'*Tormented*,' Mum rolls her eyes. Of course, it's easier to think that I'm overreacting, rather than face the truth.

'Can't you just do as he says, for a quiet life? He's not asking much.'

I'm stunned.

'You are unbelievable, Mum. Who even are you?' I say, shaking my head at her. I can't keep the look of disgust off my face, and I know my eyes are glaring like hot coals. We stare at each other, and I wonder for a moment who this woman is.

'You want me to pretend that this is all normal?'

I grab Lizzie's picture, 'Pretend this is how our life is? All pretty and colourful? Rainbows and unicorns and happy families? Because this,' I rip the picture in two and throw it at Mum, 'is bullshit!'

'My picture!' Lizzie shouts, and bursts into tears. I feel a pang of guilt, she shouldn't be witnessing this.

'Lizzie, go to your room please,' Mum tells her firmly.

'Lizzie, baby girl,' I bend down to her as she picks the torn paper up from the floor, 'I'm sorry about your picture. Why don't you go to your room now, and I'll help you draw another one later?'

'I don't want another one, that was my best one! It was our family!' She grabs her crayons and paper and leaves the room.

'Look at the problems you're causing, Kya.'

I am infuriated beyond measure. Her refusal to see things from my point of view and her lack of motherly concern, her inability to see what's right in front of her. I want to slap her. I want to cry out *Mum! I need you! I need my Mum! Why can't you be my Mum? Where did you go?* I can't do either of these things, so instead I ball my fists up at my sides, my fingernails stabbing my palms, I keep the words in my throat, won't let them out, the lump in my throat so big, the angry frustrated tears feeling like acid, burning the backs of my eyeballs.

'It's not me, Mum.' I almost spit the words out, because I can't let the emotions go or who knows what I will do.

'And who is this thug boyfriend of yours?'

'Thug?' I laugh out loud, 'Thug?'

'He threatened your father! Had him against a wall!'

'Threatened him? Father? What the? Mum, Zak pulled *him* off *me*! He had me by the throat! It was *me* who was threatened, and thankfully Zak was there!'

'Well you won't be seeing this *Zak* again. We've decided. We're not having someone like that causing even more trouble. Your father has a reputation to uphold and he can't very well be seen…'

'Father?' I shout, 'Don't *ever* refer to him as my father!'

Mum stays calm. 'He's been more of a father to you than your own dad ever has.'

'You are deluded, do you know that?' I spit. I let the tears go, tears of anger, but mainly tears of hurt. I've lost another piece of my mum. I've lost all of her. 'I can't wait to get out of here. And when I leave, just know that I won't be coming back!'

I march out of the kitchen and trip over Lizzie, who's been listening at the other side of the door. I'm too upset and mad to stop so I carry on towards the stairs but she follows me.

'Kya, who hurt Daddy?' She's right behind me on the stairs.

'No one hurt him, Lizzie. Leave it.'

'But Mummy said your boyfriend hurt him against the wall? Did he hurt my Daddy?'

I bite my tongue. I have always protected Lizzie from my

feelings towards her Dad, never vocalised what a despicable being he really is.

'Lizzie, leave it,' I say calmly as I shut my bedroom door.

She bangs on it with her tiny fists. 'I hate your boyfriend, Kya! He hurt my daddy and I hate him!'

*One day you'll understand, baby girl. One day, when you're grown up and we're best friends, I'll be able to tell you all about it.*

## Lizzie

I look at Daddy and he doesn't look hurt. He doesn't have any scrapes or bruises, but he looks so mad. Madder than ever. He doesn't look up while he's eating his sausages. We're not allowed to talk. Daddy said he wants silence at the dinner table. Maybe he has a headache. Grown-ups get them a lot. Mummy has given him extra sausages and mashed potatoes and keeps asking him if he wants more gravy. He doesn't answer, he just nods his head and she pours more gravy on. *Nice and thick, just like you like it*, she says. She gets him another drink. Mummy is really good at looking after people when they're sad or hurt. She does the same for me if I'm poorly or if I've fallen over and hurt my knee. I'm glad she's looking after Daddy.

## Kya

'So we're not allowed to even talk now?' I can't keep quiet.

Mum shoots me a look, 'Kya,' she says, warning me.

'No, Mum, it's not normal. Not being allowed to even speak at the dinner table?'

'It's called having a nice, quiet family meal,' Mum says, trying to keep the peace.

'It's called oppression,' I say, and then he slams his fist down on the table so hard the cutlery rattles.

## Lizzie

I nearly jump out of my chair! Daddy looks so angry. He's gone all red like a tomato and he's screwing his mouth up like he does when he's about to shout at Kya. I wish she wasn't so naughty to him, then we could all be happy, like in my picture, before Kya ripped it up.

'Elizabeth, go to your room please,' he says to me.

'But I haven't had my angel delight yet?'

'Elizabeth! Go. To. Your. Room. Please.'

I don't know what I've done wrong, but I do as I'm told. I don't want to make Daddy mad, even though I am sad that I won't get to have my angel delight. It was butterscotch too, which is my favourite. I sneak out of my room and sit on the landing with Bunny and poke my head through the bannister. I can hear shouting. Daddy is shouting something about *How long have you been sleeping with college boys?* Kya is shouting back *I am not sleeping with college boys.* I don't know what they mean, Kya sleeps here every night. I know, because some nights she comes and gets into bed with me. Mummy is asking everyone to *calm down* and saying *Please can we just talk like normal grown-ups.* I don't think grown-ups are normal. I think they're always angry and shouting. Daddy just called Kya a *slut*. I wonder what a *slut* is? Maybe I will ask Katy tomorrow. Now he is shouting *You are grounded until further notice* and she shouts back *I'm already a prisoner*. Daddy says if that *yob* dares to show his face at this house again he will break his legs. Then I hear the front door slam and Daddy is gone. I stay on the landing. I think that maybe if I go downstairs Mummy might let me have my angel delight now, but I don't want to move. I sit here and cuddle Bunny even tighter. The sicky feeling is in my tummy again.

## Kya

I help Mum clear the table.

'This was supposed to be a family meal,' Mum says, looking resigned.

'Maybe it's time to stop pretending, Mum?' I say softly, but matter of factly. 'This isn't the cosy little family unit you want it to be, no matter how much you keep pretending it is. Face facts.'

She scoops the gravy-covered table cloth into a ball. 'I've got to get ready for work.'

'You're actually going to work, *tonight*?' I ask, incredulous.

'Of course I am. Why would I not be going to work?'

'Mum, do you have to go to work there? I can't be alone in this house with him. It's torture, Mum. Every minute I'm on eggshells waiting for him to start on me. And he's gunning for me even more now.'

She busies herself putting the table cloth into the washing machine.

'Mum?'

She lets out a sigh and stops what she's doing. She looks at me. If she really thought about it, if she really looked inside herself, if she was one hundred percent honest with herself, if she'd take off the cloudy film that she's covered everyone and everything with, then she'd see it. She'd know.

'Mum, please don't leave me in the house with him?' I implore her. She's in there somewhere, I know she is.

'Kya,' she says quietly and then sighs, no fight left in her, 'things will calm down. He'll calm down at the social club, and you can just stay out of his way.

I feel sick. She doesn't see. Correction, she chooses not to see.

'It's not like you go there for the money, Mum. I mean, that all goes straight into the bank account that you don't even have access to because he controls it all. What's even the point?'

'Because it's something for me, Kya. It's a tiny bit of me.'

For once, she's being authentic.

'I like it there. I like the residents, and I'm good at what I do. I feel good, you know? I'm a carer, and I care for these people. Some of them haven't even got any family.'

And that, there, is my mum. The mum I know and love. She's still in there. I smile at her, but I feel sad.

'And I like the people I work with. They're my friends.'

I get it now. She has a little life there. There, she is someone meaningful. There, she is liked, respected, worth something. There, she has a little break from her own reality. I get it.

'But what about your wages, Mum? You should get to at least enjoy the rewards of your hard work? He's got loads of money, surely you should be able to keep yours and treat yourself. You couldn't even buy a new top for your work Christmas party because you had no money and he wasn't dishing out.'

'It's my way of feeling like I pay for you. I don't ever want him throwing it in my face, *again*, that he pays for you. So I contribute, and he can't throw that at me.'

And it dawns on me what she's doing, why she does it. Not only is it a tiny sliver of independence, having something for herself, a little life away from being just mum, wife or maid, she's doing it so he can't throw that card at her. Or at me. So he's not footing the bill for the daughter that's not his.

I throw my arms around her and hug her tight, we're about the same height now, and she hugs me back. We stay like this for what seems like minutes. I don't want to let go. I still need my mum.

'I know things are difficult at times, sweetie,' she says, her cheek on mine, and she squeezes me tighter. The tears are rolling down my cheeks now. 'Please, Kya, for me, and for your sister, for us all, let's just try and get on.' She doesn't say it but I know she's admitting things are really shit.

I can't do anything. I can't change anything. I can't make her leave him. I can't dictate what will happen to Lizzie when I leave here in two years, I can't control any of that. All I can control is how hard I work at school now and how I can get into university and finally leave. I know she loves me, deep down, but I'm never going to get from her what I want or need, so I just resolve to look after myself. Work hard at school, study, work the weekend at the hardware store, save my money.

## Lizzie

**M**ummy is getting ready for work. Kya runs my bath and lets me put as many bubbles in as I like. She scoops a big blob of bubbles from on top of the water and puts them on my nose and we giggle. I like it when Kya baths me. She does all the funny noises, like when she reads my stories, and she doesn't mind if I splash and everywhere gets wet.

'So your boyfriend didn't hurt Daddy then?'

'No, baby girl. They had a little argument but he didn't hit your Daddy.'

I feel happy now.

'Anyway, he's not my boyfriend,' Kya says in a funny voice and splashes me with water and I splash her and we laugh and laugh.

She rinses my hair, which smells like strawberries from my strawberry shampoo.

'I could EAT you!' Kya says and she sniffs my hair and lifts me out of the bath, and I say 'No don't eat me, don't eat me!' and I laugh and wiggle my legs in the air because she's pretending to eat me. Then she wraps me in my fluffy pink towel with the hood and we are still laughing as she scoops me up for a big fat cuddle. She hugs me extra hard tonight. She sniffs my head again, even though my towel hood is up.

'I love you so much, baby girl.' She's not laughing now. Just hugging me tight. I like it. It keeps me warm.

'Now, what story are we having tonight? Don't tell me it's the one about the bear in the cave again? We've read that a hundred million billion gazillion times already!'

'Yes!' I shout, because I love that story and a hundred million billion gazillion times is not too much. 'The bear one, the bear one!' And we laugh again and she carries me to my room.

After my story we lie in my bed, just Kya and Bunny and me, and Kya strokes my hair. She is asking me about Daddy, like has he ever done anything to me and I ask *What like?* and she says, has he ever done anything naughty to you or anything you don't like or has he ever hurt you. I shake my head. She says I must promise to tell her if he ever does anything naughty to me or hurts me or is mean to me and I tell her I promise but I don't really know what she means. We lie there in the quiet and she's still stroking my hair while I fall asleep, and after a while she says *I want your life to be different to mine* but she says it so quietly while she's kissing my hair and I'm not sure if she's saying it to me or my hair so I stay quiet because anyway I'm falling asleep.

# Kya

*Is Jane Eyre a likeable protagonist and why, or why not?* Friday
night and I'm doing school work, but there's nothing else
to do. I'm grounded. I've read the book twice now. Once for
pleasure, a couple of years ago, and now for school. I like the
book, and in many ways I feel I can relate to Jane. She lives
where she does not want to live, in Gateshead Hall, tormented
by her bully of a cousin, John. She has a lot to contend with –
oppression, inequality, hardship. She longs for a family, a sense
of belonging, safety, love. She faces exile and imprisonment in
the Red Room, a place of terror where she thinks she sees
monsters and demons. I think about what the Red Room
represents, if it is simply a symbol of what Jane has to overcome in order to find peace, happiness, belonging, love.
Finally she is sent away to a boarding school, and her life
begins. I wish I could be sent away to a boarding school. I
think about how, in those times, women were expected to be
gentle and submissive creatures, but Jane was a strong character with clearly defined goals and a tendency to push the
boundaries, question everything, challenge society. Her
sudden inheritance and resulting happy ending were not

typical for women during that time period, and under most circumstances, Jane would have been forced to maintain a subservient position, either by continuing her work as a governess or by marrying an oppressive husband. Jane's independent spirit and unwavering courage, despite what's thrown at her, makes her a protagonist to be admired and respected. *I will do my best, although it is a pity that doing one's best does not always answer.* I read this line again and again and it resonates so intensely. I have written my favourite Jane Eyre quote on a post-it note and I repeat it out loud as I read it, trying to get inside Jane's head, trying to imagine what life was like for her: *I am no bird; and no net ensnares me: I am a free human being with an independent will.*

I'm lost in my thoughts and have almost forgotten where I am when the sound of the front door closing and keys landing on the hallway table pulls me from my peaceful thoughts. I feel the knot in my stomach return, and the thought of him instantly makes me feel angry. I tense up and my skin prickles. I'm unable to feel relaxed or safe in my own home. Correction, *his home.* I hear him walking up the stairs and my hackles come up. *Know your escape routes.* I hold my breath when I hear the creak of the floorboard as his foot lands on the top step. He stops, pauses, right outside my room. I'm still holding my breath and my heart beats faster. I feel dizzy, a lack of oxygen mixed with hatred and anger. I can see his shadow underneath my door. I feel sick. *Know your escape routes.* There aren't any. I imagine bursting out of my door, he wouldn't be expecting it, and I could push him down the stairs as hard as I could. Hopefully he'd break his neck, and his body would lie crumpled and broken on the bottom step. The shadow leaves and I breathe out again. I hate living like this.

I open up messenger.

*Angry_Teenager:*

Are you home?

*Tall_Dark_Dangerous:*
Yes, is everything ok? Has something happened?

*Angry_Teenager:*
I'm ok. Don't panic. Can I come over?

*Tall_Dark_Dangerous:*
Let me think about that for a second. YES! Aren't you grounded though?

I don't reply. I close my laptop, creep down the stairs, grab my coat and leave the house. *I am no bird; and no net ensnares me.*

## Zak

I look around quickly to check if my room looks ok. Relatively tidy, clean. It's the first time she's been here and my heart is beating in anticipation. Kya, in my room. Just me and her. In my room. We've only ever been together in public, at school, in our graveyard. I grab the few loose clothes that are slung over my chair and throw them into my laundry basket, the wet towel I've just used I hang up in my ensuite. I think of Kya and what she said about feeling like she hasn't got any privacy, doesn't even feel safe in her own bedroom. I can't imagine what that's like. This is mine, and I love it. It's my cave, it holds all my secrets. It's my sanctuary, and I know no one will ever intrude. All teenagers should have privacy. Hell, all kids, no matter what age, should feel safe. It's a basic right.

## Kya

His mum is out, which I'm grateful for. I'm not ready to do the whole *meet the parent* thing. He leads me up to his room. He has the entire attic which has been made into a spacious bedroom with a bathroom included. The smell of soap and shampoo hangs in the air and I try not to imagine him in the shower. The thing that strikes me the most is that he seems so relaxed. I realise with sadness that this is normal, this is what it must be like to be a regular teenager and have friends over to your house. You can be relaxed, you can be happy, you can be yourself, you can flop back on the bed or sit on your bean bag and laugh and talk or watch TV or listen to music because it's *your* space and no one can invade it. No one can burst in and scream at you for the music being too loud, scaring your friends half to death, so they never come back. Causing such a scene you stop inviting people round because you're constantly on eggshells, waiting for an outburst, waiting for the shouting, the humiliation.

'This space is amazing.' I look around in awe. A giant framed poster of Jim Morrison hangs on the wall, there's an electric guitar propped up in the corner, and various other Doors memorabilia scattered about which must be his Dad's. He sits on the floor and motions to a giant beanie so I sit down.

'Drink?' he says.

Then I see the mini fridge stocked with cans of coke and chocolate bars, and I laugh.

'Oh my God, you could literally live up here and never come out,' I say, and we laugh, and I feel the weight of the world, my shitty world, lift from my shoulders. All thoughts of home and *him* and everything else leave me, and it's just me and Zak, listening to music, like regular teenagers.

The music is loud but it's ok, his mum is out, and even if she was here, he says it's ok, she's cool. We're talking about Jim Morrison and listening to The Doors and Zak is so vibrant, so passionate. He gets up off the floor and goes to the fridge for more drinks and turns up the volume.

'This is one of my favourites!' he says, and as the chorus kicks in he closes his eyes and stretches his arms out wide and sings to me in a joking way. I love how he's not self-conscious at all.

He does air guitar and I relax back, sinking into the giant bean bag, and enjoy his goofy performance. I grin and laugh as he jokingly serenades me. He can't sing, but his voice is sexy, deep. He emphasises the words *touch me babe* and looks into my eyes imploringly, and I know there's a flirty message there. He stands still in front of my bean bag, hovering above me, closes his eyes, one arm outstretched to the side, the other arm bent, hand on heart, and he slows down for the chorus, his voice deep and gravelly, singing that he's going to love me till the heavens stop the rain and the stars fall from the sky.

'You're mad, you know that?' I laugh.

'I know, but you love me for it.' He winks at me and I

melt. He holds out his hand and I take it, and he pulls me up to my feet.

'I'm exhausted,' he laughs. 'Lie down with me.' He's confident, self-assured, sexy as hell. He leads me to the bed and flops himself down, and I lie next to him. There is nothing else. Only me and him.

# Zak

It's so easy to be around her. I get her. She gets me. It's like we've known each other forever. We lie down on the bed and my breathing starts to slow. I'm out of breath from jumping around and singing. We lie on our backs and talk.

'So why was Jim Morrison buried in Paris? What was the connection?' Kya asks. She's been reading the book I gave her.

'He loved the place. He used to love walking around Père Lachaise, that's the cemetery, so they buried him there. It's the largest cemetery in France, and the most visited necropolis in the world. It's always been my dream to go there, walk around it myself, try and feel what he was feeling, and visit his grave of course. He's buried close to Oscar Wilde and Chopin you know. I've saved up enough money to go, it's just *when*, and *who with*. I look at her, my eyes telling her I already know it's her I'll be going with. 'My Dad always wanted to go,' I add. 'So I want to go for him.'

'Tell me about your Dad?' she asks.

I've never spoken to anyone about him before, girls I mean. His memory is too precious to me. I've never bared my soul enough. I pause, trying to figure out how I can sum up the fifteen years I had with my father, what he was like, what he meant to me, before he died. I roll over onto my side to face her, prop myself up on one elbow. She does the same.

'I'm scared I'm going to forget what he looks like.'

Kya takes my free hand in hers and squeezes it gently.

'I'm scared I'll forget the sound of his voice, the sound of his laugh, the sound of my mum and dad laughing. They were always laughing.'

'Were they really in love?'

'God, they loved each other so much. They'd been together since high school. Mum worked at the cinema on the popcorn stand and Dad used to go to the movies every Saturday just to see her. He would watch films he hated, but it was the only excuse he had to go and see her. He was too nervous to ask her out, and eventually his best mate, Bill, threatened that if Dad didn't hurry up and ask her out, then he would!'

Kya smiles. She's a good listener.

'It was their favourite story. I'd heard it a hundred times, but I would always ask *What happened next?* I loved listening to them tell it.'

'So what happened?'

'Mum would tell how he was so nervous. She always had a twinkle in her eye when she reminisced about it. She would spend ages doing her hair and makeup just in case he'd come to the cinema. One night he came in and went over to her stand to buy popcorn. She could see his mates giggling in the background. He was so flustered he dropped his change all over the floor. Mum would laugh as she relayed the punchline we'd all heard a hundred times: *In the end I said, for heaven's sake, are you going to ask me out or what?* So he finally plucked up the courage and said, *Would you like to go out with me?* And I would always ask, *What did you say, Mum?* And she would say, *I said,*

149

*about time, mister!* And we'd all laugh and laugh. I loved hearing that story. Mum and Dad would laugh while they told me, holding hands at the dinner table and looking into each other's eyes. I loved that they still loved each other so much, after so long. We were such a happy family, so tight, so normal.'

'And then what happened?' Kya asks.

I pause, lost in my thoughts. *And then*, I say, but only in my head, *that's when I started high school and started hanging around with the Piper brothers, and everything changed.* I know I'll have to tell her the truth eventually, just not yet.

## Kya

I lose him for a moment, as he stares into nothing, lost in his own thoughts. He doesn't answer my question about what happened, so I say something else.

'Sounds like they were really in love?'

He comes back. 'Yeh, they were. They really were. I want what they had together.' He looks at me, squeezes my hand. I want to hear more about his family, but he changes the subject.

'Tell me about your dad?' he asks. I wonder about my Dad for a second. Is he a good man? What does he look like – is he tall, short, big build? Do I get my green eyes and dark hair from him? I could walk right past him in the street and never even realise it, and neither would he. Maybe he lives on the other side of the world. Does he ever think about me? Does he have a family? Do I have brothers or sisters out there? Maybe he's dead. Mum doesn't know anything about his whereabouts.

'He left my mum when she was pregnant with me. She won't even tell me his name.' I shimmy over to him and nestle my head onto his chest as he moves flat on his back. It feels so natural. 'I have these dreams,' I tell him, 'about a humming-bird.' He strokes my hair. 'The dreams are always different, but the hummingbird is always there.' I think of all the pretty colours and try to put them into words. 'The colours are like nothing I've ever seen before, and I don't just see them, it's as if I'm feeling them. I know that sounds crazy, but the colours, they're electric, so vivid, so vibrant. Words can't do them justice. Its feathers are somewhere between blue and green, bright teal, sometimes turquoise, and shades of purple, violet, lilac. The colours seep into my soul. And I get this really strong feeling, like they're there to give me a message. The feeling I get, sometimes it's pure joy, then it's terror, as if it's a warning sign, and I feel this strange dread. But it's always there, the hummingbird. All the pretty colours.' I realise I'm only whispering, half in a trance.

'Our mind's unconscious wandering says a lot about our personality, apparently.'

'I wonder what hummingbirds say about me?'

'I think you're an INFP, like me.'

'A what?' I laugh.

'An INFP – introversion, intuition, feeling, perception. It's one of the personality types identified on the Myers-Briggs Type Indicator. I've always known we were the same one.'

I'm intrigued. 'Ok, go on then, so what's my, sorry *our* personality type?'

'We enjoy drifting into deep thought, we enjoy contemplating the hypothetical and the philosophical more than the other personality types do.'

'So far, so true,' I agree. I shuffle a little closer to him and he responds by moving his hand up and down my back, in a gentle, stroking movement. It sends shivers up my spine.

'We're open-minded, imaginative, creative, although we tend to be quiet and serious, considering all things carefully.

We're analytical. We can be introverted, and can have a tendency to withdraw into hermit mode, becoming detached.'

'I like hermit mode,' I say.

'We may appear serene and gentle at first glance, but can become fiery and intense if provoked.'

I can definitely be fiery. And intense.

'So, what if you get two of these personality types together? Is that not a recipe for a fiery disaster? Or a pair of insular hermits who think they're smarter than everyone else?'

'I think they would come together and make each other better and happier than they ever were when they were alone.'

I like the sound of where this is going.

'Underneath the armour we're hopeless romantics. We can sense when we meet someone special and are going to bond with them on a deeper level.'

Now I don't know if he's talking about INFPs still, or describing us. His hand is still travelling, slowly but firmly, up and down my back.

'We're passionate. Our emotions run quickly, and when we fall, we fall fast, and hard. And,' his hand on my back stops, 'INFPs are good in bed.'

I lift my head up to see if he's teasing me now, and he's grinning wickedly at me. I prop myself up on one elbow and he does the same. Now we are lying facing each other. He is so self-assured. I wonder if he's been with other girls. He must have. How many? I know nothing of his old life, before he moved here. I try not to think about him with another girl, it seems unnatural to think of him as anyone else's but mine. Mine. I want him to be all mine, and now is the time to let him know I am his.

'So what makes you so sure INFPs are good in bed?' I talk softly. I've never really flirted with anyone before, but there's something inside me right now that makes me want to drive him wild. I catch him glancing at my mouth, and I bite my bottom lip teasingly. I know it's working.

'Intimacy is important to us, and we're passionate when it comes to sex. It's about the bond, the connection, not just the act.'

He's staring hard into my eyes, and it's as if he can see directly into my soul. We're so close I can feel the heat in the small space that sits between us.

'We're generous lovers, putting the pleasure of our partner first.'

His hand starts trailing my back again, but this time it goes lower, and hovers around the base of my spine, trailing a circle with his fingers. The electricity between us is palpable. And right then I know I can't hold back any longer. I am under his spell. It's time to show him that I am his, and he is mine.

## Zak

*Vorfreude* – a German word that describes the joyful anticipation that comes from imagining future pleasures. I've thought about this word a lot recently. The anticipation is intense. She sits up, slowly, without breaking eye contact, and I move with her, sitting up too. We face each other.

'I could stare into your eyes all day and still believe they are the most beautiful in the whole world.'

She stares back at me, and her eyes say it all, *I'm ready, kiss me now.*

## Kya

This is the moment – the moment between us staring into each other's eyes and our first kiss. This is the moment where the world stops. The only thing between us is the anticipation of his lips on mine, a moment so intense, it pulls us closer. A moment so intense it hangs thick in the air. A moment so perfect. I will him to kiss me. He places his hand gently on my cheek and I close my eyes, and then I feel it, for the very first time, his kiss, his lips on mine. I know in that moment I have well and truly fallen, and there's no going back.

## Zak

Our lips fit together like the whole world was created purely so we could have this moment. Her lips are softer than I imagined. We kiss slowly, gently, my hand on her cheek, her hand resting gently on my leg. I let her lead the way. She pushes her lips harder onto mine, she sits up straighter to free the arm she is resting on, and she places it on the back of my neck, pulling me closer to her. She's kissing me harder. Our breathing quickens. My hand slides from her cheek and around the back of her head, underneath her hair, softly taking a handful. She pushes her body closer to me and I want her, so much, but I don't want to rush this. We kiss harder, more urgently, and then, as if we're both thinking the same thing, we pull back simultaneously. And it's then, when it's over, that I realise that actually, it's only just beginning.

## Kya

'A re you ok?' he asks, looking into my eyes intently, his hand resting lightly on my cheek again.

My heartbeat starts to return to its normal rhythm, although my lips are still tingling with pleasure. *Am I ok?* I'm more than ok. I am more ok than I've ever been in my life.

'I don't ever want to leave.' My voice is a whisper.

'Then don't,' he says, kissing me once, softly, on my lips. I close my eyes and feel myself melt again. 'Stay.'

## Lizzie

I am eating my choco pops at the breakfast table. Mummy and Daddy are waiting for Kya to come home, because she didn't come home last night. Daddy is mad and keeps saying she never should have gone out because she was grounded, and she is even worser for staying out all night. Mummy keeps saying *Please, just let it go, she's sixteen, and she sent a message to say she was staying with a friend.* Daddy says he doesn't care if she sent a message. Mummy says we can't keep her prisoner. I stay quiet and stir my choco pops until the milk can't get any browner. I can't eat them though, because my tummy hurts again.

## Kya

I *am no bird and no net ensnares me*, I tell myself, as I turn my key in the door. They are all sitting at the breakfast table when I go in. Mum says *Hi* and Lizzie runs up and hugs my legs. He barely acknowledges me, but he's not kicking off, which is a good sign. I don't want to risk jinxing it, but dare I say, all is ok? I sit at the breakfast table with them, just to make sure everything is, actually, all ok. We make small talk. Mum tells me about her shift and how Mr Arnold still thinks she's his daughter. She's trying to lighten the mood, make things normal, but it's forced. Lizzie makes me watch her stir her cereal, *Look how the milk goes brown!* I go up to my room and flop down on my bed. I'm not at work until this afternoon. My phone beeps. *Zak.* I smile, remembering how we just held each other all night. Fully clothed, on top of the bed clothes, all night, just talking, him stroking my hair as I burrowed into his chest. And of course, we kissed. Those soft, beautiful kisses. I read his message: *She was beautiful, but not like those girls in magazines. She was beautiful, for the way she thought. She was beautiful, for the sparkle in her eyes when she talked about something she loved. She was beautiful, for her ability to make other people smile, even if she was sad.*

*No, she wasn't beautiful for something as temporary as her looks. She was beautiful, deep down to her soul. She is beautiful. F Scott Fitzgerald.*

I grin, and flop back onto my bed, clutching my phone to my chest and grinning from ear to ear. This is what it's like then, to feel like a normal sixteen-year-old girl.

## Zak

I'm trying to study. There are only a few weeks of the school year left and I've got one last assignment to finish, all about free will and determinism, and exploring if the two are mutually compatible. Is it possible to believe in both without being logically inconsistent? My mind is distracted with thoughts of Kya. I am burning the incense she gave me – Nag Champa – and it smells of her. I think of how she lay in my arms all night, all the things we spoke about, and of course, I think about her kiss. I think about the dreams she told me about. I open up my browser, type in *hummingbird* and hit search.

I message her. I know she's online, studying before her shift at the store.

*Tall_Dark_Dangerous:*
In native American culture, hummingbirds are thought to be healers and bringers of love, luck, and joy.

*Angry_Teenager:*
Have you switched Philosophy for Ornithology?

*Tall_Dark_Dangerous:*
I was curious.

*Angry_Teenager:*
What else have you deciphered? PS I'm imagining you crouched in a bird hide with a pair of binoculars.

*Tall_Dark_Dangerous:*
If a hummingbird appears near you (let's assume this means in your dreams too) they are reflecting the positive side of life to you. They are symbolic. They want you to let go of the big stuff and find joy in the small, simple things. They are tireless in their pursuit for finding sweetness, and they want you to enjoy sweet things too. PS I'm imagining you in my bed again.

*Angry_Teenager:*
You're distracting me!

*Tall_Dark_Dangerous:*
I want to distract you…

*Angry_Teenager:*
You seem to forget that my hummingbird, whilst incredibly beautiful, is either imprisoned or mercilessly decimated?

*Tall_Dark_Dangerous:*
Ok, so I don't know what that means. Maybe it means your resilience will overcome any obstacles that you are enduring at the moment.

*Angry_Teenager:*
I hope you're right.

*Tall_Dark_Dangerous:*

I'm always right…

*Angry_Teenager:*
Cocky.

*Tall_Dark_Dangerous:*
I was right about us, wasn't I?

## Kya

It's been a couple of weeks. I haven't stayed over since that first night, but I go over some evenings and we hang out, listen to music, read together. And kiss. Mum doesn't know I'm with him, she thinks I'm hanging around with Chloe Darley again. It's nearly the end of school and I'm thinking about exams. My predicted grades are good and I've been provisionally accepted to do the A levels I've chosen. It's all coming together! I'm keeping my head down at home, working hard on my studies, things seem ok. I've met Zak's mum and he's right, she's cool. I can see where he gets his features from – she's stunning, with a sharp jawline, prominent cheekbones and dark eyes, just like his, and she radiates warmth. I think about his dad and what a wonderful man he sounds like, and I imagine how they must have looked as a family, the three of them, all beautiful, happy, laughing, and I feel a pang of heartache for them both.

'What are you kids up to, then?' she asks. 'Taking a break from your studies, I hope? You've both been working so hard.'

I smile. She's right, we have.

'You deserve a break. Here, treat yourselves to a chippy tea.'

She gives Zak a twenty. We don't need any more persuading.

## Zak

We sit on the wall, eating our chips with tiny wooden forks. Kya feigns horror at the amount of salt I put on my chips, and I laugh at how she absolutely drowns hers in vinegar. We are both *excess* personified. We finish our chips, put the paper in the bin and sit a while, just chatting.

'Oh, shit,' she says.

'What?' I ask, but then I see him, pulling up alongside the curb, staring out at us from his big flash estate car. I look at Kya and although her face stays stony, I feel her tension. He opens the passenger window and leans over the empty seat. His beady little eyes glare at Kya, his gingery moustache twitching as he speaks.

'I told you you weren't to see that boy again.' He glances at me briefly. 'Is this who you've been spending all your time with?' he snaps, not waiting for an answer. 'Get in the car!' he snarls.

'No.' Her answer is confident, firm, her face unfazed.

'I beg your pardon? I *said*, get in the car!'

'And *I* said no.'

'You have to the count of three to get in this goddam car, young lady…'

'She said, she's not getting in the car!' I say on her behalf, my adrenaline pumping already. He ignores me and stares straight at her, his mouth pursed.

'If I have to get out of this car…'

But before he can finish his sentence, I'm on my feet and flying towards the open window.

'You'll what?' I yell, fury seeping out of my very pores. I imagine opening the door and dragging him across the passenger seat and out onto the pavement. But he doesn't answer me, because he's already speeding off, tyres screeching as he does so. I want to beat him to a pulp. Kya takes my hand in hers, and eventually my breathing slows.

## Kya

I've learned that everything in life is temporary, so when things are going well in life, you have to enjoy it because it won't last. The last few weeks have been the most normal few weeks I've had, and the happiest. It figures that the bubble was always going to burst.

Zak walks me home and is loath to leave me at the end of the street, but I've got to face whatever it is I've got to face when I walk through that door. I somehow persuade him I'll be ok, and he reluctantly lets me walk away. He doesn't see the tears stinging my eyes.

They're sitting at the kitchen table waiting for me. I notice Mum's in her uniform. She's not meant to be on shift tonight.

'So you decided to grace us with your presence, then?' he snarls.

'I do live here,' I say, trying to keep the cockiness out of my voice. I want this to be over with as quickly and painlessly as possible.

'I called Chloe Darley's mother,' Mum looks at me, disappointment etched on her face. He looks smug, as if Mum's finally realised what a thoroughly evil teenager I am.

'She said she's not seen you for months, and what a shame it was that you and Chloe stopped hanging out together.'

I'm silent as I sit down at the table. There's nothing to say. They know I've been seeing Zak, not Chloe, there's no point trying to deny it.

I ready myself for the shouting and yelling from him, but it doesn't come, although I can see the wrath in his eyes. Instead, Mum gives me a lecture about betraying trust, acting up, causing problems, setting a negative example to *Elizabeth* etc. The way they're talking, anyone would think I was a drug taking, knife wielding, thieving delinquent, not a sixteen-year-old girl who studies damn hard and just wants to have a normal life and hang out with her boyfriend. I sit quietly and take it. If this is all I have to do, then fine, I'll sit here and listen to what a disappointment I am and how ungrateful I am because they've been so fair and so lenient with me. Some of it stings, like really stings, and part of me wants to defend myself, shout out the truth, but what's the point? They won't take it on board. They won't change. I won't let them make me feel worthless but I hate them for it. I hate Mum for it. I sit and take it, the criticism, the insults, because I just want this over with so I can go to my room.

The lecture is over, and Mum takes a breath.

'Are you working tonight?' I say, calmly.

'Yes I am. I'm covering for someone. Did you listen to a word we said, Kya?'

'Yes, I heard every word.' I heard every painful, disappointing word.

'Well, what do you have to say for yourself?' he snaps. He doesn't like to see me calm, unruffled. He wants blood.

'What do you want me to say?' I am calm. 'I'm a terrible teenager and a huge disappointment?' I shrug my shoulders. I speak quietly, apathetic, emotionless.

'We told you we didn't want you seeing that boy.'

'His name is *Zak!*'

'I don't give a damn what his name is, sunshine, you're not seeing him, and we'll make damn sure of it this time.' He's pointing his long finger at me and his moustache twitches as he snarls the words. I notice he has a piece of food in it, which repulses me.

'You don't get to control who I see. I'm sixteen years old for heaven's sake. How are you going to stop me from seeing him?'

'Because you're grounded, indefinitely, until you start respecting our rules, and if it means being grounded for the entire summer holidays then so be it. And this time, we'll make sure you won't be sneaking out.'

'Grounded? You're treating me like a child!' I say, incredulous. I've risen to the bait, and he looks pleased now.

'Mum?' I ask, desperately.

'We both agree that's what's best, Kya.' She can barely look at me as she speaks.

'Best for who? What purpose is that going to serve?'

'You have your exams coming up. Your mother and I think it's best you focus on them, instead of getting distracted by some boy. You'll thank us in the long term.'

He doesn't care about my education, this is just a good excuse to control me, and a good way to get Mum to agree to it. I glare at him, and he glares back.

'I literally cannot wait till the day I can leave this house for good!' I shout at them, but it just plays into their hands. *There she goes, unruly, moody teenager, and here we are, the poor innocent parents that have to put up with her.* I have never felt so powerless and frustrated.

# Zak

*Tall_Dark_Dangerous:*
How's it going over there?

*Angry_Teenager:*
Grounded indefinitely. At least until exams are over.

*Tall_Dark_Dangerous:*
What does your mum say?

*Angry_Teenager:*
She agrees. He's got her wrapped around his little finger.

*Tall_Dark_Dangerous:*
Will they be able to enforce it?

*Angry_Teenager:*
Apparently so! They're going to make sure one of them is always in, just so they can be certain I don't sneak out. I'm surprised they've not put a lock on my bedroom door.

*Tall_Dark_Dangerous:*
They can't do that?!

*Angry_Teenager:*
What can I do about it? Apart from climb out of my bedroom window in the middle of the night and risk breaking a limb.

*Tall_Dark_Dangerous:*
Maybe they'll come round after a few days. Let the dust settle.

*Angry_Teenager:*
Maybe. Maybe not. All I know is I hate it here. I hate it so much. And I hate him.

*Tall_Dark_Dangerous:*
You'll get through this, Kya, and you'll come out on top, I promise. You're strong. Transform your anger into a force for good, use it to fuel your studies. Remember what Nietzsche said, *He who has a why to live can bear almost any how,* and, *That which does not kill us makes us stronger.*

I know what he's trying to do, and I love him for it, but Nietzsche quotes won't help me now. I wonder what Jane Eyre would do.

## Lizzie

I can hear Kya's music in her bedroom. I've never heard her play this music before. It's very loud. I hope Daddy doesn't get mad. He gets really mad if he can hear Kya's music.

## Kya

I scroll through my playlist and find The Doors. I listen to the music and somehow feel closer to Zak. I get what he means now, this is why he listens to music to feel closer to his Dad. I lie on my bed and close my eyes, letting the music wash over me. I think back to our conversation about how much Zak wants to visit Père Lachaise Cemetery in Paris, and how one day we will go there together. I imagine us there together now, nothing in the world, just me and him, no one else. No one to tell me what to do, no one to control me. Just me and him, hand in hand, walking through the cemetery, then later, lying on a bed together just listening to music and talking and talking until eventually the world stops spinning. I'm ripped out of my daydream by *him* bursting through my door, red faced, eyes wild, and before I've even sat up and taken stock of what's going on, he's ripped my speaker out of the plug socket. The music is cut.

'What are you doing?' I'm shocked, and anger wells up inside me, but I have to swallow it down. He's on the warpath.

'I'm taking this away so the rest of the house doesn't have

to suffer this deplorable rubbish!' he shouts, holding up my speaker, and I can see the spit flying out of his mouth.

'You can't take my things!' I exclaim, rage overpowering my fear.

'You're not listening to this!' He waves the speaker at me and heads to the door.

I get up off my bed and rush over to try and grab my speaker but he pushes me back, hard, and before I know it, he's out of the door and has slammed it shut.

'You've ruined my life!' I scream as loud as I can, and I don't care if he comes back in and screams back at me or even hits me because right now, at this moment, an intense rage has overtaken me and it is all encompassing. If I kept a baseball bat in my room this is the part where I would lose control and smash everything up. Instead, I grab the photo frame that sits on my desk, steal a glance at the picture of me and mum at the seaside when I was seven, before throwing it at the door. It smashes, but it doesn't satisfy, doesn't extinguish the raw anger that's burning me. *How can he do this?* I grit my teeth, clench my fists, thump my pillow, but nothing satiates, and a fresh swell of resentment towards my mum, towards him, shoots through my veins. My chest starts to constrict and I realise I can't breathe properly. I feel like someone is sitting on my chest, and I slump down on the floor and remind myself to *breathe, just breathe, in, out, in out, this will pass, it always does.* Eventually my heartbeat slows, my breathing returns to normal and the pain in my chest dissipates. Once the anger has passed I feel the true weight of my sorrow, but there's absolutely nothing I can do about it, so I hug my knees to my chest and I rock slowly back and forth, marinating in misery.

## Lizzie

I can hear Kya crying in her room. I want to go and see her and kiss her like she kisses me when I am sad or hurt, but Daddy said I have to stay away from her because she is very naughty. She's never naughty to me and I only want to cuddle her. I take Bunny from my bed and I put him outside her door. I hope she finds him soon. I always feel better when I cuddle Bunny.

## Kya

I've cried and cried and I feel pretty sure I can cry no more. I am resigned. I am a dry autumn leaf, powdery, light-weight, just waiting to blow away or disintegrate.

I open up messenger and type.

*Angry_ Teenager:*
I wish you'd killed him that morning.

## Zak

I'm worried about her. What's going on? She hasn't replied. If he lays a finger on her I swear I'll kill him. I could have killed him that morning. I imagine my hands around his neck, like they were. I can see his soulless little eyes looking back at me, smell his rancid coffee breath. I can feel the muscles in his neck pulsing underneath my fingers. I could have killed him. I could have squeezed harder. His internal muscles would swell, pushing on his veins and arteries, cutting off his blood flow. It wouldn't take a lot of pressure to occlude the jugular vein, stopping blood from passing through and starving his brain of oxygen. He'd have about ten seconds before unconsciousness hits. He would struggle violently at the terrifying realisation he can't get any air, though unbeknown to him the struggle would cause more damage to his neck. The pain would be unbearable, and his eyes would bulge, blood vessels bursting underneath his skin. Fifty seconds later and death is becoming a very real possibility. He knows this and loses control of his bodily functions, piss streaming down his leg. His brain now starved of oxygen, he becomes hypoxic, reaching the point of irreversible asphyxiation. Even if he survived this, he'd be brain dead, a cabbage. But I wouldn't stop. I'd keep my hands squeezed tightly around his neck for another few minutes just to make sure, then I'd let his lifeless body flop to the floor, and he would torment her no more.

Eventually she replies.

*Angry_Teenager:*
*But still, like dust, I'll rise* – Maya Angelou.

It takes another five messages back and forth for her to convince me she's definitely ok. Eventually I fall asleep, and I dream of strangling him. The demons in my head goading me, *Do it! Do it! You've killed before, you can do it again!*

## Lizzie

I'm fast asleep but I wake up a little bit when Kya gets into bed with me. She found Bunny, and now he is in between both of us. She snuggles up and we fall asleep. I like it when she sleeps with me.

## Kya

I'm a mere few weeks away from the exams I've been working so hard for. I haven't seen Zak as I'm officially on study leave, so no more walking to school. I've spent days getting distracted by thoughts of him, not being able to focus. Wanting him, needing him. This is exactly what I wanted to avoid, becoming reliant on someone. I need to focus on myself, on my revision. I haven't got any real work done for days and I can't jeopardise my exams, I just can't, there's too much riding on them. I can't get lost in thoughts of Zak anymore. I need to focus, protect myself. I'm going to end it, at least for now. I need to. I can't wait any longer. Better to rip it off like a plaster. Be short, blunt, firm. If I think about it, it will break my heart, so I bring up the barriers and resume Ice Queen mode. I open up messenger and keep my message simple.

## Zak

I haven't seen her for days and I'm missing her so much. She's quieter than she normally is, not replying to my messages as much. I know she's busy studying and I don't want to distract her, but God I miss her. And then she messages me and my whole world comes crashing down.

*Angry_Teenager:*
I can't do this anymore. Us. I need space to focus on exams. I'm sorry. Please understand.

*Tall_Dark_Dangerous:*
What are you saying, Kya? I won't get in the way of your studies, I'll give you all the space you need! Please don't say that it's over between us?

*Angry_Teenager:*
I'm sorry.

*Tall_Dark_Dangerous:*

I don't believe you. I don't believe this is what you want! Please don't push me away, Kya.

I freeze. A feeling of utter dread creeps over me, permeating my pores, soaking into every cell. *Please don't push me away Kya. I need you. I need you as much as you need me. You just don't know it.*

She doesn't reply. I check messenger every half an hour for the rest of the day, and still she doesn't reply. Her barriers are up. Her impenetrable barriers. And there's not a damn thing I can do about it.

## Kya

I've turned off messenger so I can't see the messages I know he'll be sending. I know I will have broken his heart and I can't bear to think of it, so I'm not going to log on. *Self protection*, I remind myself. *It's for the best.*

# Zak

I leave it for twenty-four hours. I won't hound her, it'll only push her further away, but I need her to know that I love her and I won't give up on us.

*Tall_Dark_Dangerous:*
I'll give you all the space you need, and I am here whenever you are ready. We didn't find each other by accident, the universe conspired to bring us together. Whatever our souls are made of, mine and yours are the same. We're meant for each other. I won't give up on you. I won't give up on us. x

We're meant to be together, I know it, I feel it in my bones, and people who are meant to be together will always find their way back to each other, no matter how far they wander. I know the universe looked down on us and said *'It's them. Those two. I'll give them both a difficult path, but then they'll find each other, and when they do, they'll experience a love like nothing else. A love that transcends the earth, the universe, all of existence. And nothing else will matter, as long as they have each other.'*

## Kya

A week in. I'm numb inside. Everything I do is mechanical, robotic. I wake up, I study, I sleep. I can't even say that sleep is my only relief, because it's not. I toss and turn and I dream of Zak, I dream of failing my exams, I dream of the hummingbird and all the pretty colours, I dream of monsters lurking in the graveyard. I don't want to eat, I have no interest in anything. The heavy brick I feel like I'm carrying around on my chest makes breathing difficult, and I feel lightheaded. I don't want to turn on messenger because I know there will be messages in there from Zak. I can't think of him, it hurts too much, so I block it all out, better to stay frozen inside. I think about messaging, just to let him know I'm ok, let him know I'm still here. All that's left of me anyway. I don't want to feel, but even when I feel nothing, I feel it completely.

## Zak

*Tall_Dark_Dangerous:*
*I'm so tired of being here.*
*What is this life, if it is not with you?*
*I've had a taste of paradise, and now I can't forget.*
*If you truly want to part, I could almost accept that.*
*Almost.*
*But you don't.*
*So I can't lay it to rest.*
*I can't give up, knowing there's a chance, knowing you feel the same.*
*Because I know you feel the same.*
*A tragic waste.*
*Your presence lingers here, like a ghost that won't leave me alone.*
*At the same time the emptiness suffocates me.*
*Your face haunts my dreams.*
*I feel your touch on my skin, only to wake and find you not there.*
*My wounds won't heal, the pain excruciating.*
*There's so much that cannot be erased.*
*The times we had together. The conversations.*
*There's still so much we have to do, see, experience together.*
*When you screamed I helped you face your demons.*

*When you cried, I wiped away your tears.*
*I love you and I'm not afraid of your darkness.*
*Because I've seen your light, and it's more beautiful than anything in this world.*
*You showed me your demons.*
*You never saw mine, but still you chased them away.*
*I needed you just as much as you needed me.*
*I still need you.*
*Stop fighting.*
*Come back to me.*

I press send, but I know it will sit in her inbox, unread, just like all the others.

I feel myself sinking, and I don't want to go back to that place. I feel panicky. My demons are stirring. *It's your fault he's dead.* I rub my eyes. I haven't slept properly for days. *It's your fault your dad is dead!* they scream. *No! No!* I tell them. *That's not true!* I can't go back to that place. The place where I believed life was more painful than death, death being a welcome release. I try to fight sleep because I don't want the dreams to come back. But I feel myself falling, falling, *Don't fight it!* I don't want to fall, not like I did before, because if I sink, I won't be able to save her.

## Kya

I log onto messenger. Twelve unread messages from *Tall_Dark_Handsome*. I can't read them. I log out, close my laptop, cry myself to sleep.

## Zak

I fall into a fitful sleep and start to dream. I'm floating in the air, somehow watching myself down below. I'm sitting at my desk in my room, writing. I sense suffering in the air, sadness, pain, despair, and I wonder what the *me* in the room is going through.

*'If you don't know how to die, don't worry; Nature will tell you what to do on the spot, fully and adequately. She will do this job perfectly for you; don't bother your head about it.'* – Montaigne

I watch as I write this out onto a piece of paper and stick it to the wall above my desk. I take a clean sheet of paper, crisp and white, and I start writing. I'm writing a poem. I watch from above, as the *me* below writes. I can't see the words, but I don't need to, I know every word already. It's my final poem. My goodbye.

*It is strange, how people fear death.*
*They fear it. They fear pain.*

*But I find life hurts a lot more than death.*
*Death is the precise moment when life ends. And that is painless.*
*Death will welcome me into its arms.*
*Death will be a rest.*
*Free from the pain that is life.*
*The pain I endure.*
*I can't stay.*
*The truth will drive me into madness.*
*Whispered voices in my ear.*
*I close my eyes and will them away, but they don't stop.*
*And they bring the pain. All the pain.*
*This is the only way.*
*I say goodnight.*
*I won't be here much longer.*
*I'm not afraid.*
*I want atonement.*
*I cry for deliverance.*
*It ends here.*
*I pray for the black.*
*Sweet blackness.*
*Death before my eyes.*
*I'm sorry, Mum.*
*I'm so sorry.*

*Don't do it!* I'm willing the *me* in the room. I know what's coming. He's folding the poem up, leaving it neatly on his desk. He walks into the bathroom. I'm screaming at him to stop, but nothing's coming out of my mouth, no sound. He can't see me, can't hear me. I can hear him emptying the bag in the bathroom but I can't get to him. I hear the glass bottle smash against the sink. And then I am no longer hovering above, watching the scene below, I have returned to his body. I am him. I am sitting on the cold, hard floor, back against the bath, broken glass all around me. I have a thick piece of glass in my hand. I don't feel any fear. I'm not scared. I feel a strange kind of peace, the calm pleasure of no longer being able to feel, anticipating the welcome relief of death, the finality of it all. I take a breath, and then it's done. *Why am I not dying?* This wasn't meant to happen! *Where is death?* I long for the blackness, but it doesn't come, I can only feel pain. I tried to kill the pain, but this has only brought more. So much more. I panic. Sweat runs over my skin. I lie there, dying, but it's not coming quickly enough. It's not painless. I feel the pain of every ounce of life flowing out of me. I'm pouring, pouring, a crimson river on the white tiles. Crimson regret. *I'll be there soon, Dad.* I'm dying. Praying. *Please, quickly.* Bleeding. I remind myself that at the point of death, the pain will be over. But death doesn't come. I'm trapped, neither dead or alive, imprisoned in some sort of middle existence. I can't get there. I can't get back either. I'm all alone. Hysteria sets in. I'm screaming *I'm so sorry!* Am I too lost to be saved? Am I too lost?

❦

I wake up screaming, my heart beating out of my chest, my bed sheets are soaked, and in my half-asleep state I expect to see them drenched in crimson blood, but I realise it's just sweat. *Just a dream*, I tell myself, *just another dream.*

I haven't had the dreams for a long time. I've been doing fine, working hard to keep the demons at bay. I'm terrified of them coming back. I know now I have to let her go. I open up messenger, and I quote Jim Morrison. The words sum it up perfectly.

*Tall_Dark_Dangerous:*

*This is the end, beautiful friend. This is the end, my only friend. The end of our elaborate plans. The end of everything that stands. The end.*

I press send. It could have been something so beautiful.

## Kya

It's eerily calm at home, like the calm you feel before a storm. I'm anxious, as usual, thinking about the volcano that's been dormant for a while, knowing it won't stay passive indefinitely. Or maybe it will. Maybe living like a zombie, soulless, staying in my room studying twenty-four seven, is enough not to wake the slumbering beast. Maybe this is what it takes to have a quiet life at home? But am I willing to give up my soul, my voice, my being? Become *Mum*. I think it's annoying him, my being obedient, submissive. He has no reason to yell at me. There is absolutely nothing I am doing that I could possibly be condemned for. Instead, he ignores me, excludes me, pushing me out of conversations at dinner, ordering pizza just for him and Lizzie when Mum's at work. I realise I haven't eaten today so I take a break from studying and go to the kitchen to get some toast.

## Lizzie

'Kya, do you want some of my choco pops? These ones are the best!'

Kya is wearing the black and white pyjamas Mummy got her for Christmas from me. I helped choose them. The top has a little red love heart on it and it makes her look like she has really big boobies! Daddy must like her pyjama top too because he is staring at it. Kya pulls her cardigan around her and gives Daddy a really bad look.

'I've lost my appetite,' she says, sounding really cross, and stomps out of the room. What did I say wrong? Maybe teenagers don't like choco pops.

## Kya

**F**ucking creep. I don't know what's worse, the red-faced tirades, the yelling, the cutting remarks, the sarcastic comments, or the fact that he now stares at my chest like some sort of beady-eyed pervert. I thought I was imagining it at first, but it's happened a few times recently. I have actually caught him looking at my breasts, and not in a cursory way. In a lecherous way. He makes my skin crawl, and the unease washes over me, making my skin prickle. I find myself double checking the lock on the bathroom door when I'm in there, keeping my eyes on the bedroom door when I'm getting dressed in my own room, going to sleep with pyjama bottoms on, making sure the string is tied extra tight. My hackles are up. Living in a constant state of vigilance is exhausting.

## Lizzie

My tooth finally came out today! Me and Mummy wrapped it in tissue paper and put it under my pillow before she went to work. She said if I go to sleep nicely then the tooth fairy will visit and leave me a coin. Kya comes into my room. I love it when we have sleepovers in my room and she cuddles me to sleep but I tell her she can't tonight, because the tooth fairy might not come if she is here. She looks a bit sad, but she says it's ok and goes back to her room. I squeeze my eyes shut and try really hard to get to sleep.

## Kya

I think about moving my chest of drawers in front of the door while I sleep, but they're too heavy. I think of Zak, and how protective he was of me. God I miss him. I could message him but I'm too scared. Has too much time gone by? Would he forgive me? Would he think I just want to pick him up again now that school's out and exams are over? I'm too nervous to open messenger and read my messages, in case there are any in there from him. What if they're angry messages? I know I hurt him, ditching him like that, and the thought of him in pain sends a stab of anguish through my own heart. Maybe he's moved on. Maybe there's a message in there telling me to go to hell, or telling me he's found someone else. I can't bear to think about it. Instead I read Jane Eyre cover to cover.

## Lizzie

I am going on my very first sleepover tonight, to Aunty Sarah's. She is Daddy's sister and she lives with my Uncle Robert and my cousin Grace and she has a baby called Noah. We are going to have pizza and ice cream and I am sleeping in Grace's room and I can't wait! I have packed my best pyjamas, the ones with the glitter stars on, my unicorn slippers, my toothbrush, and Bunny. It is great being five, when you get to go on sleepovers.

## Kya

'Why are you so worried about Lizzie staying at Sarah's? Sarah is amazing with her, and she gets on so well with Grace. She'll have the best time.'

'Do you *have* to go to work, Mum?'

'Yes, Kya, I have to go to work. What's all this about?'

I shrug. I can't put my finger on it. I know Lizzie will be fine. It's me that's not fine. It's me that's nervous, and I don't really want to admit that, if I really think about it, I am nervous about being in the house on my own with him tonight. My stomach is knotted, and I have a sense of foreboding. Something feels off. Every fibre of my being is telling me that something is wrong. It's like when it's been really hot for days, stifling, and eventually the sky goes dark grey, the storm brewing. It hangs in the air, you know the thunder's coming, can smell the rain before it's even started falling. And you wait. You wait for the loud crack.

## Kya

I light an incense stick and the smell of Nag Champa fills the room. I take a deep breath, but it doesn't calm me like it usually does. Mum put my speaker back in my room a few days ago, and I'm listening to The Doors, although I'm careful not to have it too loud. It's getting late but I'm not tired. I don't want to go to sleep anyway. I open my book, close it again. Can't concentrate. Then I hear footsteps on the stairs and I stiffen up. I pray he just goes to bed. The top step creaks, as it always does, and my door handle goes. I jump up, as he opens the door and looks in.

'Can you knock?' My voice is louder than I expected it to be, and I instantly regret it. I pray he will just go away, leave me alone.

'It's 10 o'clock. Turn that off.' He motions his head towards my speaker.

'It's hardly loud,' I say, trying to keep the exasperation from my voice. But he doesn't need goading, I've already given him enough reason to start on me.

'If I say it's too loud, then it's too loud, now turn it off! Or would you rather I took it away again?' The vein on his temple starts to throb, his eyes glisten with the anger he can't control, his mouth puckers up under his moustache. I bite my lip and will myself to stay quiet. Diffuse the situation. But I know, deep down, these things never just diffuse.

'Answer me! Would you prefer it if I took it away again?' He rips the plug out of the wall again and turns to stare at me, waiting for my answer. If I stay quiet, I'll be ignoring him which is ill-mannered, rude, insolent, therefore playing into his hands. If I answer, I'll say something wrong or my tone will be uncivil. We both know I can't win. He's spoiling for a fight, and he won't stop until he's got one.

'Please can you just leave my room,' I say, desperately trying to keep the shakiness out of my voice.

'*Your* room,' he sniggers. '*Your* room? I think you've forgotten whose house this is. You don't appreciate anything, do you? You just laze around, listening to trashy music and burning these ridiculous sticks!' He takes my incense stick and stubs it upside down on the plate, extinguishing it. 'I do not want you burning these sticks, or listening to this music, or…'

'How about I stop breathing as well?' The words spill out of my mouth, and I realise I'm shaking. Dread cripples me as he stops still and looks at me, malice in his eyes.

'Stop breathing?' He's walking towards me, 'Stop breathing, you say?'

I step backwards but he grabs me by the throat, his thick fingers around my neck. I remember what Zak told me and I kick out as hard as I can but I miss my target and kick him in the thigh instead. It stuns him enough to let go of my throat, but he raises his hand and slaps me with all his might. My cheek burns like fire and I scream out, but no one can hear me. Now he's pushing me, pushing me backwards onto the bed. He's shouting something but it's all a blur. I'm screaming at him to get off me as he pushes me down on the bed, his hands pulling at my pyjama bottoms, trying to get them down, and I'm thankful I did the knot extra tight as I kick out at him with my legs. I can smell his body odour and he says something about *teaching you a lesson if you think you're so grown up*. I struggle against his weight, and he has hold of my wrist so tightly it hurts, holding it above my head, but my other hand is free, so I stiffen my two fingers straight like Zak showed me and jab them as hard as I can into his eye. He shrieks, and I have a split second to roll off the bed and run for the door.

'You little bitch!' he screams, but I don't look back. I slam my bedroom door shut behind me and my heart's racing as I bolt down the stairs as fast as I can, even though my legs feel like jelly. He's out of my room, screeching at me to *Get back here* as he chases me, but I don't look back, praying the key is in the front door and it is, and somehow with my shaking hands I turn it and I'm out of the door. It's raining hard but I'm out, and I run like hell. I'm running and running and I can't think straight and before I know it, I'm at Zak's house, throwing stones at his bedroom window and screaming his name, and it's not until he opens his window and his face contorts as he says *Jesus Christ*, that I crumple to the ground in a heap. I don't stop to think what I must look like in my pyjamas, or register that the grass is completely sodden.

## Zak

I'm physically shaking as I take the stairs two at a time, my heart pounding. I'm thinking all sorts in the time it's taking me to get from my room to the front lawn. I know instinctively he's done something to her. Has he hurt her? Worse? I run to Kya and throw myself down by her side, searching for signs of him. Nothing obvious. The grass is soaking but I don't care. I throw my arms around her and she buries herself in my chest, sobbing. She's shaking. She is only wearing pyjama bottoms and a strappy vest top. I want to hold her for as long as she needs but I also need to see her face. I push her back gently and take her face in my hands. She winces. She has a huge red mark on her left cheek.

'Jesus Christ, Kya, what has he done to you?' I feel sick. 'We need to get you inside.'

I look around once more, then help her up and lead her inside.

'It's ok, Mum's out,' I tell her, and she nods her head. I hold her elbow with one hand, my other arm around her, and lead her up to my room.

I stand and look at her in the light of my room. Her cheek

is starting to bruise already. I search her face for other marks. I hold her arms up and inspect them. She has marks around one of her wrists.

'Kya, what the hell has he done to you?'

She bursts into tears again.

'Please tell me he didn't…' I can't even say it. If he has, I will kill him.

She shakes her head. 'No. No, he didn't. But I think he might have, if I hadn't got away.'

My whole body fills with relief. It takes everything I have to push the anger to one side, to ignore the urge to go and find him and beat the crap out of him until he's lying still on the floor in a crumpled, bloody mess.

'You're soaking. Here, come in here.' I lead her into the bathroom and get her some towels. 'I'm going to run you a bath and get you a hot drink.' She grabs hold of my sleeve, not wanting me to go.

'It's ok, Kya, you're safe here. You won't ever be going back there. You're safe here. I'm not going to let anything happen to you, ok?'

'I'm so sorry,' she cries and buries her head in my chest. 'I'm so, so sorry, Zak.'

'Shhhh,' I stroke her hair, it's wet, but it smells just like Kya. 'You have nothing to be sorry for.'

'I missed you so much.' She holds me tight and somehow the world feels right again. Me and her.

'I missed you too. More than you'll ever know.' I lift her face up and hold it gently in my palms. She isn't wearing makeup, her trademark black eyeliner gone. Her eyes look even more beautiful than I ever imagined they could look.

'But you're here now, and that's all that matters. I will never let anyone hurt you ever again, I promise.'

## Kya

I lie back in the bath, sink down as far as I can go, and let the hot water engulf me. The lights are dimmed in his bathroom, and the room is filled with the smell of the bubble bath that he found in his mum's bathroom. I feel strangely calm. The peace that returns after the storm. I've cried so much I feel worn out and washed up. I sense him outside the bathroom door.

'I've made you a hot chocolate. Shall I leave it out here, or…'

'You can come in.'

He comes in and he's not quite sure where to look. It's sweet.

'It's ok, you don't have to look away.' The bath is so deep and so full of bubbles the only visible part of me is my head. He looks at me, relieved, and sits down on the mat by the side of the bath.

'How are you feeling?'

'Better now,' I smile. 'I must look a mess.' I realise he's never seen me without my makeup on before.

'You have never looked more beautiful,' he says, and that

feeling I always got when I was around him returns, the feeling of connection, lust, love, but this time it's accompanied by a twinge of sadness and a sharp pang of guilt. How did I ever let him go? What was I thinking?

'I'm so sorry, Zak. For everything. I know I hurt you.' I look at him, and pray that as he looks into my eyes he can see it's the truth, that I always felt this way about him, that I was just scared. I want him to see right into my soul. I'm ready to bare it all.

'Shhh, it's ok, I understand.' He kneels up and takes the hand I've just offered. I smile, remembering how perfectly my hand fits in his.

'I can never go back there,' I say, calmly.

'You won't ever have to go back there, I promise.'

'What am I going to do?'

'We'll figure it out. But you don't need to think about it tonight.' He squeezes my hand, and I smile at him. I believe him.

'Thank God Lizzie wasn't there,' I say, almost to myself.

'Where's Lizzie?' he asks, and I tell him. Then I tell him everything that happened. Bit by bit, recalling every sickening detail like how I could smell his body odour as he yanked at my pyjama bottoms. *What was he going to do to me?* And he listens. I cry again and he squeezes my hand. I can see the anger in his eyes as I talk, but still he listens. He listens, and I talk, until the water goes cold.

## Zak

I try to keep the emotion from my face as she tells me everything. How she's exhausted herself, numbed her own soul, just to keep him from flaring up. Then tonight. He could have seriously hurt her. Or worse. I think of what could have happened and bile rises in my throat. She must sense it, because she squeezes my hand and assures me that she's ok, that she had a lucky escape. I run the hot water to warm the bath up, and resume my position by the side of the bath. She closes her eyes and I study her face. Her black hair glistens with wet as it hangs down one side of her face. The other side of her neck is exposed and as I look at her creamy skin something inside me stirs.

'You're looking at me. I know you are.' Her eyes are still closed but a smile plays gently on her lips.

'I can't help it. It's been a while. I need to make up for lost time.'

'I'm a mess,' she says quietly.

'I told you, you don't look a mess, you are beautiful.'

'No, I mean I *am* a mess. Inside.'

'You're a masterpiece.'

'I'm like broken pottery. All angry cracks, smashed and broken.'

'That's where real beauty lies, Kya, in the cracks.'

'Unfortunately, we live in a world where people are judged on their cracks.'

'Well, that says more about the person judging than the one being judged. Kya, don't be ashamed of your fractures. The people who matter, they'll see the true beauty of how you put yourself back together again, time after time.

'You always know what to say, don't you?' Her eyes glisten as she looks at me so intensely, 'I don't know what I'd do without you.'

I ache to kiss her.

'I don't know what I'd do without you,' I tell her back. 'You think I've saved you, Kya, but really it's you who saved me.'

'You don't need saving. You're the most together person I know.'

'I might seem like it now, but I haven't always had it together.'

'What do you mean?'

'Kya, there's something I've not told you. I know we always said no secrets, but this is big.'

A look of unease clouds her face, and she loosens her grip on my hand.

'There's something I have to tell you, about the real reason we moved here.'

## Kya

I'm not sure I can take anymore trauma tonight. *Please, God, don't let this be bad. I can't lose Zak, he's all I've got right now.* He looks nervous. He rolls up his black sleeves and holds his arms out to me, palms facing upwards. I gasp out loud at the thick red scar that runs the length of each forearm, elbow to wrist. He looks embarrassed but I know he's baring his soul to me. I don't know what to think, I'm lost for words and so instead I just stare, the scars so red against his pale skin. How have I never known about his scars? He always wears long sleeves, but then so do I.

'Oh, Zak,' I say, reaching out to take his hand again. 'How? Why?' I want to sit up but the frothy water is my only modesty. 'Why did you keep this from me?'

# Zak

'I was afraid, I guess. And I didn't want to scare you off!' She squeezes my hand and smiles sympathetically, then urges me to go on.

'I sank into a depression after Dad died. He had a heart attack. It was my fault, or at least I thought it was at the time. Still do sometimes. I don't know. I was fifteen and I went off the rails a bit, started hanging round with the wrong kids, smoking pot and staying out late. I don't know why but it felt kind of good, going against the grain, not conforming, being a bit daring. We were always so close as a family, but I started distancing myself from Mum and Dad, staying out later, keeping secrets, stealing cash to buy pot. Dad knew what I was doing. He was exasperated with me.' I can't look her in the eye, I'm too ashamed, but I want to be totally honest with her.

'Look at me, Zak,' she says quietly, and nervously, I do.

'It's ok, you can tell me. No secrets, right?' She smiles, encouraging me to go on.

It gives me strength. I take a breath. 'We had an argument, I'd taken money from his wallet. He knew it was me but I denied it. I lied to his face and stormed out. I went to a party at a friend's house, two brothers I knocked around with, not good sorts. Their parents were away. Dad called me on my phone, he was furious. I got dozens of missed calls from my parents but I ignored them, drank some more, blocked it out. Then the messages started coming from Mum, worried messages, and I knew something was wrong.'

I haven't spoken about this to anyone apart from my old grief counsellor. It feels painful again, raw. Kya squeezes my hand reassuringly.

'He'd had a heart attack. I knew it was my fault, the stress I caused him.'

'Oh, Zak. Surely it wasn't that, I mean…' she trails off.

'They did tests, said he had undiagnosed hypertrophic cardiomyopathy, and that it couldn't have been my fault, it was inevitable. But I couldn't handle it. Couldn't handle the guilt. Couldn't handle the fact that the last interaction we had was us arguing because I'd stolen money off him.' I let the silence hang between us for a minute. I look down at my arms and I feel Kya look too. 'I couldn't handle the pain, the guilt. I didn't know how to cope. I wanted out. But I guess I didn't do a good enough job.' I laugh quietly, trying to lighten the mood.

'How old were you?'

'Sixteen, just. I had counselling, and I know it's not my fault now, his heart would've given out at some point anyway. But it's the way he went – the timing, after our row. I can't bear his last thoughts of me being disappointing ones. And I miss him, you know.' I move around on the floor, crossing and uncrossing my legs. Trying to keep my voice steady and calm, trying to keep the tears from brimming over. 'I've been squeaky clean since. I don't drink, don't smoke. I work hard. I look after my mum, try and be the best son I can be. The best thing I can do is be the finest version of myself so if he's out there looking down on me, he'd be proud. It's as if I'm making it up to him in some way.'

I can't hold back anymore, and I start crying.

She stands up in the bath. Instinctively I stand too, and she pulls me towards her, embracing me, holding me so tight, and I don't care about the wet or the bubbles, in that moment the world stops spinning. I don't even process that she's naked in front of me and how, under normal circumstances, I'd have given anything for that to happen. At this precise moment we are both bare in different ways, and I let everything go and I let her hold me as I cry, and she cries too. I don't want her to think I'm weak, but at this moment, we couldn't be closer, we couldn't be more connected. The universe won. It conspired, and here we are, together, unbreakable.

## Kya

I hold him close. I don't even care that I'm naked. He is stronger and more beautiful to me now than he ever has been, if that's even possible. I pull back, looking at his t-shirt that's now soaked through.

'You're wet,' I laugh, apologetically.

'You're incredible,' he says, not averting his eyes from my face. He turns around and grabs a towel, wraps it around me, his eyes never leaving my face. He is too polite. I want him to see me naked, I want us to both be as naked as we can be together, naked in body and soul. I reach for his hand and lift his arms up to my lips, and I kiss the red scars that run the length of his forearms.

## Zak

'You are more beautiful and courageous to me now, than ever,' she says, and I know she means it. I feel it. A feeling of pure relief washes over me. Like a weight's been lifted. We go into the dimly lit bedroom and we stand and face each other. She holds my hands and lifts my arms up, then looks at me. Her hair hangs wet on her shoulders and glistens.

'Don't be afraid of your scars,' she says. 'They're proof that you've come out stronger. Stronger than the pain that consumed you, the pain that made you want out.'

'I don't think I could love you more if I tried,' I say to her, and I kiss her lips gently. She starts to shiver.

'I'd better get you something to put on.'

## Kya

I curl up in his arms in his bed and stroke his beautiful chest. I'm wearing his favourite Jim Morrison t-shirt and he is wearing nothing but shorts. He strokes my hair and I stroke his chest, broad and muscular, *so this is what it feels like under his top.* I think about his scars. I wonder if it would be easier if I had scars, on the outside I mean. Validation of some sort. You can't see the scars on the inside. Sometimes they're the worst ones. Only you know they're there.

'Everything will be fine in the end,' he says quietly, 'I'm certain of it. If it's not fine yet, which it isn't, then it's not the end. And we know it's not the end yet, but it is near. And it will all be fine. You'll see.'

## Kya

We fall asleep, wrapped up in each other. Nothing else matters, just that we are together. Before long I'm dreaming, and the hummingbird comes again. I'm outside, standing in the middle of a field of flowers. I stretch my arms out to the side and feel the softness of the long grasses that surround me, and I touch the delicate flowers, shades of pink and purple and orange. I can smell their pretty scent. The hummingbird hovers in front of my face, and it's so peaceful out here, wherever I am, that I can hear the sound of its wings beating as it hangs in the air, its eyes looking right at me. Sunlight shimmers on its beautiful feathers, colours of turquoise turning into teal, then emerald green, then violet, lilac and lavender. I can feel the sun on my face and hear the birds in the background. *It's going to be ok*, I think to myself. *This is a sign. It's all over now.* Then, all of a sudden, the sky turns black, heavy clouds closing in. The sound of the birds tweeting in the background disappears and it turns cold. I fold my arms and hug myself to keep warm. A sense of unease grows in me, and although the hummingbird still hovers in front of my face, it is no longer a friendly messenger of hope and joy, it's foreboding. *It's not over*, I realise, *there's more to come*. The tiny bird tilts its head to one side and my gaze is drawn to its long, needle-like beak. It's the last thing I see before it pecks my eyes out.

## Zak

I've spent a good deal of the night awake. Partly because my mind has been going over my amazing plan, partly because I just wanted to lie here and hold her, watch her sleep. She was exhausted and fell asleep quickly, I watched as her breathing slowed. I held her in my arms and stroked her damp hair. I can see daylight breaking through the gap in my curtains. She's stirring, almost fitful, like she's having a bad dream. She wakes with a start, breath heavy, and her face says it all.

'Shhh, it's ok, I'm here, you're safe.' I reassure her as she looks around, startled, gathering her senses, then she relaxes. 'Bad dream?'

'You could say that,' she says, lying her head back down on the pillow, worry etched on her face. 'What time is it?'

'Nearly seven. Don't worry, there's no rush to get up. Hey,' I stroke her face, 'you ok?'

She smiles, but it doesn't reach her eyes. 'Reality's hitting me now. I've got to deal with this, somehow. Mum finishes work at eight. I need to go and see her.'

'You don't have to worry about that yet,' I say, smiling, sitting up now, dying to tell her my plan.

'What do you mean?' she says, eyeing me suspiciously.

'You don't have to worry about a thing, at least not for a few days.'

'Okaaay?'

'You need to get some clothes and things from your house though. Will he be going out today?'

'Yeh, he'll be going to pick Lizzie up this morning from her sleepover. Tell me what you're planning?'

'Oh, and you'll need your passport, or at least some ID.'

'Oh my God what have you done?'

'We're going to Père Lachaise, baby!'

She looks at me like I've lost my mind. Perhaps I have.

'I've planned everything in my head! I told you I've been saving for this for years, and I've got more than enough for both of us. We can take the Eurostar and get a hotel for a few nights. Kya, this is our chance – we're going to Paris! There's no better time – school's out, you need to get away to process things. This is the perfect opportunity! Please say yes?'

'You're crazy, you know that?' She laughs, and I see the sparkle return to her eyes.

'I'm crazy for you,' I say, 'But then you already know that.'

## Kya

He tries to persuade me to stay in bed a bit longer, but I need to get to the care home and see Mum before she leaves for home. I throw on the pyjamas that have dried crispy on the towel rail in the bathroom overnight, splash my face with water and run my hands through my hair. Zak comes back upstairs with hot, buttery toast.

'You are literally the perfect guy, aren't you?'

'I'm pretty special,' he winks at me cheekily and my stomach flips.

'So how am I going to get out?'

'It's ok, Mum's leaving for the hairdresser's in a minute.'

I'm relieved.

'So, you know the plan?' He asks me one more time.

'Yes!' I laugh, pulling on the jumper he's handed me. 'I know it inside out, you've told me fifteen times!'

He smiles at me, that cheeky, sexy, irresistible smile. My stomach flutters at the thought that I will be in a hotel room with him tonight, in Paris.

'I'll go and see Mum, and I'll be back here by eleven.'

'And I'll get everything booked while you're gone. I still

can't believe it, we're actually going to Paris!' he says, pulling me to him. 'I can't believe that, not only am I actually going after all these years, but I'm going with *you* – that's just out of this world!'

His grin is infectious and I don't think I've ever seen him so enlivened. 'Well, I'm going to get going then. The sooner I go, the sooner I get back.'

He walks me downstairs and stops at the front door, turning serious. 'Kya, be careful,' he says, holding my face in his hands.

'I will,' I assure him. 'I know what I have to do.'

'Promise me you won't go near that house if he's in? And promise you'll look out for his car when you go to your mum's work? He might want to get to her before you do.'

This thought has already crossed my mind. I know how he works, like a child wanting to get his story across first. I wonder what he'll tell her, what lies he'll make up about me.

'I promise,' I say, and I stretch up to kiss him, and he kisses me back and it takes everything we've got to tear ourselves apart.

'I'll be back before you know it,' I tell him, as I walk out of the door and scan the surrounding area for signs of him or his car.

'I won't rest until you're back here, safe with me,' he says.

I smile at him and I turn and leave. I know he's watching me walk away, and knowing how much he loves me fills me up with strength.

## Zak

It doesn't take long to book everything – train tickets to Ashford International, Eurostar tickets, and a hotel. I've booked us into a small place close to Père Lachaise Metro Station, which couldn't be more perfect. I keep thinking how yesterday I felt empty yet full of pain and sorrow, and tonight I'll be in Paris with Kya, it's surreal! It goes to show the difference a day can make.

I check my phone. She's only been gone forty minutes, but I can't sit still, I'm on edge, so I grab my coat and leave the house. She'll be at her mum's work now, and I wonder how it's going – will she believe her? Tell her she's sorry and that she'll leave her wanker of a husband? Somehow I can't see this happening. I'm worried she'll bump into him, so I head off in the direction of her house, telling myself I'll just stay close by in case she needs me. My phone is in my hand, waiting in case she calls. I turn the corner of her street, thinking perhaps I'll just hang around on the corner, but then I see him, closing the front door, locking it. Before I know it, I've put my phone in my pocket and I'm running, running towards him with fire and fury as he walks towards his car, his suit jacket thrown over his arm, briefcase in one hand.

'YOU!' I shout, my heart pounding, my blood pumping, my adrenaline off the scale. He looks up and sees me running towards him and he looks like a rabbit caught in headlights. I don't stop, I simply plough into him and knock him to the ground, and before I know it, he's on his back on the grass and I'm sat on top of him, one hand on his throat, pinning him to the ground, the other arm raised, fist clenched, ready to strike down on his face.

'What on earth...' he croaks, a look of shock and terror on his face. My grip is tight. Not tight enough to choke him, but tight enough to keep him immobilised. My fist is poised but I exercise self-control. I can't risk ruining our Paris plans by getting arrested for battery. Or worse.

'I know what you did!' I spit, between clenched teeth.

He looks petrified, but tries to play the innocent. 'I can explain. It's not what you think. Just let me…'

I tighten my grip on his neck and raise my fist a little higher and he flinches underneath me. 'Don't give me your bullshit!' I shout, and then I realise the neighbours are gathering in their gardens. I hear a lady whisper *Call the police, Derek.*

I look up at her standing there in a white towelling dressing gown.

'Yes, go on, call the police, and tell them I'm holding down a rapist!'

The woman gasps. More neighbours are gathering. I hear whispers of *Oh my gosh it's the councillor* and *What has he done?* as he squirms underneath me trying to get out, but I'm too heavy, too strong for him. He tries to talk, to defend himself, but I motion my fist like I'm going to punch him and I shout at him, 'Shut the hell up!'

'That's right,' I look up at the crowd that has gathered

around. 'He's a monster. Your beloved councillor is a bully and a monster. Isn't that right?' I look at him, tears prick his eyes. 'He's an abusive monster. He's tormented his step-daughter for years. Bullied her, hit her, humiliated her. And last night he tried to rape her!' More gasps. 'So go ahead, call the police, they can deal with him. I want everyone to know what he's done!' I look down at him, his face has gone puce. 'Everyone in town will know what you really are. You're done for, you fucking bastard! Done for!' I get off him and stand up, resisting the temptation to kick him as hard as I can in the ribs. I don't need to hurt him, I know karma will do its job. It's unforgiving, and it will get him in the end, I have no doubt.

'Do with him what you will,' I say to the handful of people who are still watching, open mouthed. I look down on him quivering on the grass. He tries to get up but he's shaking so much.

'Look at you, typical bully, pathetic and cowardly. And now everyone knows exactly what you are and what you've done.'

He looks nervously at the people around him, who are looking down on him with shock and loathing.

'I can't bear to look at you.' I turn and walk away.

## Kya

Mum is surprised to see me turn up at her work, but the look on her face soon turns to dread.

'Meet me outside by the car, I'll just finish up.'

I wait outside, nervously looking around for his car in case he shows up. I feel sick, and I don't know what to expect. I'm not hopeful that she'll even hear me out, let alone swear her allegiance to me, tell me she's going to leave him. I know her first thought will turn to the inconvenience and the stress of it all, *I don't need this right now*, and *Why am I always in the middle?*

She comes out of the building and it's not long before I'm proved right. I don't get the reaction I want, in fact I'm not even sure she believes me. She's not making excuses for him, but she's silent as we drive home. I know what she'll be thinking: *She's exaggerating, such an overactive imagination, why can't they just get on?*

'Stop at the end of the road,' I tell her. 'I'm not going near the place if he's there.'

But his car has gone. We pull up and I notice the neighbours across the road peeking out of their curtains. The couple next door are getting into their car, and although they say hello, they look at us strangely and don't quite make eye contact. I tell Mum of our plans to go to Paris and she doesn't do anything to try and stop me. I'm sixteen anyway, she can't. I go to my room and hurriedly throw some clothes in my backpack, some toiletries, my passport, my bank card. My heart is racing. *What if he comes home now?* I feel the nausea rising and growing.

'So I guess that's it then,' I say, 'I'll be off.'

'You know you can't run away forever, Kya?' She says, quietly, and for a moment I feel sorry for her. Her eyes are red from crying.

'I know. But where do you suggest I go right now? What do you suggest I do, huh?'

She stares at me and her silence speaks volumes. She isn't going to fix this for me, she's unable, for whatever reason, to fix it for me, and the pain of this cuts deep, like a sharp knife slicing through my flesh. I stand up tall and remind myself that I knew this would be the case. I grab my stuff and open the front door.

'Text me, Kya, I need to know you're safe.'

Strange how she needs to know I'm safe, yet doesn't go out of her way to keep me safe at home. I nod halfheartedly.

'Bye, Mum,' I say, and I see the tears well up in her eyes again.

'And, Mum? Make sure Lizzie is safe.'

She half laughs, 'She's my daughter, Kya, why on earth would I let her be anything but safe?'

Now it's my turn to stare at her, silently. The realisation of what she's just said dawns on her and I don't need to say it, *I'm your daughter too, Mum, and you didn't keep me safe.*

## Zak

The train to Ashford International only takes half an hour, and we sit holding hands, grinning at each other giddily, neither of us quite believing we're actually doing this. I own up about going to the house and threatening him. She's shocked at first, worried about what might have happened, but then she relaxes and a satisfied smile breaks across her face.

'I actually wish I'd seen it.'

Her smile quickly fades and I know her thoughts are turning to what's going to happen after this. 'Don't worry about things yet. You're free now, we can go anywhere, do anything! Mum gave me some extra cash and told me to look after you. We'll figure the rest out. Let's just be in the now.'

She smiles and lays her head on my shoulder and I breathe her in. Before we know it, we're on the Eurostar heading for Gare Du Nord, Paris.

## Lizzie

My sleepover was the best! We had pizza and ice cream and me and Grace watched a movie and we had cookies and milk then I slept in her room. Aunty Sarah said I can come again soon. Daddy isn't speaking on the way home and he has his angry face on. We get home and Mummy is sitting at the kitchen table crying and I run to her and she hugs me but Daddy sends me to my room and I try to say something but he shouts really loud and I run upstairs crying. I can hear Mummy and Daddy shouting really loud. I hear Daddy say he will take me away and Mummy will never see me again and will she be happy then? I hug Bunny tighter. Where is Kya? Daddy comes into my room and takes my pull-along trolley from the top of my wardrobe and starts putting my clothes in it.

'Come on, Elizabeth, we're going somewhere.'

'Where are we going? I don't want to go anywhere without Mummy.'

He ignores me and keeps putting clothes in my ladybug trolley.

I'm crying but he drags my hand and I can't keep up with

him on the stairs and I nearly fall. I shout at him to wait but he ignores me. Mummy is crying in the hallway and she shouts at him *You're not taking her anywhere!* and then it happens, he hits her in the face really hard and she falls to the floor. She's not moving and I'm screaming and shouting *Mummy!* but she doesn't hear me and Daddy carries me out to the car and I'm kicking and screaming but he puts his hand over my mouth and fastens me into my car seat. He drives off and I want to go back to Mummy and I tell him I haven't got Bunny and he says *We won't need Bunny where we're going.* He is driving so fast and I'm scared we're going to crash and I'm crying *Daddy, I don't want to die!* but he just drives faster.

## Kya

We arrive at Gare du Nord and make our way to the hotel. It's late, and we're tired. We grab a cheese baguette and a can of Coke from a street stand, check into our hotel, and fall asleep fully clothed on top of the bed covers, both of us exhausted.

## Zak

The air is crisp as we walk down Boulevard de Ménilmontant towards Père Lachaise.

'Here it is, the largest Parisian park and cemetery.' I gaze around in wonderment, still not quite believing we're here. We walk hand in hand, blending in with all the other couples taking a romantic stroll through the sprawling park. There's something dreamily romantic about this place with its elegant landscaping, luscious plants, and fanciful funerary art. We walk slowly and stop to admire a stone sculpture of a couple reunited for eternity, a sobbing widow, a soldier in the midst of battle, and a man cradling his wife's head.

'I didn't expect it to be this big!' Kya is astonished. 'I wonder how many people are buried here?'

'Nobody can say for certain, but it's estimated to be anywhere from 300,000 to 1,000,000.'

'It's incredible. I can see why you wanted to come here!'

It's even more perfect than I imagined it would be. We visit the grave of Chopin, hearing it before we actually see it, his virtuosic music playing from a speaker someone has brought along, alerting us to its whereabouts. I point out the stone statue of Euterpe, the muse of music, who appears to be weeping over his grave. I talk nonstop, regurgitating facts I've memorised from years of researching this place. Kya's eyes sparkle as I tell her about the Polish soil that was sprinkled over his coffin, and how his heart was taken back to Poland and enshrined at the Holy Cross Church in Warsaw.

We walk for hours, stopping excitedly at the resting places of some of the most influential writers, painters, musicians, and politicians in history – Victor Noir, Molière, Édith Piaf, the two great lovers Abelard and Heloise, whose bones lie together. Most of the graves are bursting with colour from all the flowers that have been left.

We admire the stone angel with huge outstretched wings that adorns the tomb of Oscar Wilde. We marvel at the lipstick kisses and the graffiti containing messages of love that covers the stone, the flowers, letters, and various other unusual gifts that have been left.

And of course, we save the best for last, and my skin tingles with anticipation as we approach Jim Morrison's tomb.

'He wanted to be buried near Oscar Wilde. He idolised him,' I tell Kya. 'This is one of the most visited graves in the cemetery.'

The air is filled with the unmistakable strains of "Light My Fire" as fans gather round and sing out the iconic Doors song, and a security guard hovers nearby, ensuring it remains respectful. My heart physically swells in my chest cavity and my eyes fill with tears. *I made it, Dad. I made it here for us. I hope you're here with me.* Kya wraps an arm around me and we stand and stare, soaking up the atmosphere, enjoying the love and adoration that oozes from the dozens of devoted fans that flock around us. People leave flowers, poems, photos, candles. Some sit and raise a beer to their idol. A colourful chewing-gum-covered tree stands close by, and we watch as people stick their gum to it. I tell Kya it's a sign of independence and a flouting of authority, hallmarks of Morrison's life. There are padlocks or 'love locks' that have been fixed to nearby steel barriers and I wish I'd had the forethought to bring one for us to leave.

I read out the Greek inscription on the tomb,

KATA TON DAIMONA EAYTOY.

'What does it mean?' Kya asks.

'Literally translated, it means *according to his own daimon*, but it's interpreted as *true to his own spirit.* Perfect huh?'

## Kya

It's the end of the most perfect day. We laugh and talk over steak frites at a cosy little restaurant down the road before heading back to our hotel and showering the day off. We must have walked miles. I left my phone in our room on purpose, not wanting to be contacted by Mum, so I check it briefly but it's out of battery so I throw it back onto the table. I like the feeling of being uncontactable, enjoying my current world that consists of only me and Zak, even if it is only temporary. Something hangs in the air between us tonight, an electricity, an expectation, two lovers in Paris, a double bed in a hotel room. Last night we were exhausted, but tonight we are energised. I sit and gaze out of the window while Zak showers, and as he emerges from the bathroom naked from the waist up, drying his wet hair with a towel, I quiver. I walk over to him and reach up, placing my hands on his shoulders before running them gently down his lean, shapely arms. I move my hands to his chest, tracing them down over his taut muscular stomach.

'Take me to bed,' I whisper, and he picks me up and

carries me to the spacious bed, laying me down gently, and if there's only one thing in this world I'm sure of, it's that I want him now, and tonight I want to lose myself in his love, wholly and completely.

## Zak

We've spent the whole night exploring each other and I can't decide which part of her I'm most in love with. Although we've hardly slept, I'm still feeling electrified. I curl up behind her, my arms wrapped around her, and kiss the back of her neck softly. She is the most incredible person I will ever know.

## Kya

It couldn't have been more perfect. *He* couldn't have been more perfect. We curl up together, finally about to give in to sleep, him cradling me from behind and kissing my neck so softly. I pull his arm tighter around me and I whisper, so quietly I'm not sure he even hears me, '*I never want to go back.*'

## Zak

I wake up first and watch her for a minute before creeping out of bed quietly. I stretch and go over to the window. The streets of Paris below us are already alive. We have a whole day and one more night ahead of us and I can't wait to explore the museums and galleries today. I sit in the chair by the window and watch her as she sleeps. I've never seen her look so peaceful. She is unbelievably beautiful, the shape of her naked body under the white cotton sheets, and I could watch her for all eternity. I don't have a clue what time it is so I reach for my phone to check, and my heart momentarily stops beating – seventeen missed calls and three voicemails from Mum. I've been here before, this amount of missed calls and messages from her. It fills me with dread.

## Kya

I wake up and automatically feel the space next to me but it's empty. I sit up and he's there, sitting on the chair next to the window, holding his phone to his ear, a look of utter shock on his face.

'Kya, you need to call your mum.'

## Kya

I'm shaking like a leaf and I can't get a grasp on what's going on, Mum is crying and I can barely make out her words. All I hear is *He's taken her, Kya! He's taken Lizzie!* My stomach lurches. I have to get home.

## Zak

We sit in silence on the train, fear has rendered Kya motionless. There are no words I can use to make this better, all I can do is keep my arm around her, remind her she's not alone.

'It's my fault,' she whispers to herself, barely audible.

'Kya, this is *not* your fault,' I say, trying to get her to look at me but she stares blankly ahead.

'I've run off on some romantic little jaunt to Paris and all this time Lizzie's been kidnapped by a crazed lunatic. What if her life's in danger? What if he does something to her, Zak?'

She's shaking now and people are starting to look at us. I feel so protective of her, and I shoot a warning glance at the man opposite who quickly and sensibly goes back to reading his paper.

'I'll kill him, Zak. I'll kill him if he hurts her.' And with that she sobs and all I can do is pull her closer and hold her tighter.

## Kya

Z ak's mum is waiting for us at the station. She hugs Zak briefly then grabs me in her arms and hugs me tight.

'It will all be ok, Kya. They'll find them, I'm sure. Come on, let's get you back to your mum.'

I force a weak smile and get into the back of her car. Zak gets in next to me and I realise that, in a past life, I would have hated someone wanting to be so close to me all the time, but now, and with Zak, I like how it feels. His mum twists round to talk to me before she sets off.

'Kya, you need to prepare yourself, sweetheart. The police are at your house, and social services, and they're going to want to talk to you.'

I nod, and Zak squeezes my hand.

'And, Kya,' she pauses, a look of pain and sympathy on her face, 'there's something else.' She doesn't know how to say it. 'I'm afraid he hit your mum, before he took off. Her face looks pretty bad, but she's ok, it's just bruised, but I want you to be prepared.' And I don't really register the bit about how the paramedics checked her over and gave her the all clear because I've got my head in my hands and I'm heaving loud, heavy sobs. I've never been so terrified in all my life.

## Zak

W e pull up at Kya's house and the place is swarming with police. She unfastens her seatbelt and leaps out of the car before Mum's even parked up and turned the engine off. I walk through the open front door, my mum at my side, and Kya's in the hallway with her mum. They're hugging each other and sobbing. My mum makes tea while Kya's mum paces the room, the police reassuring them that they're doing everything they can to find Lizzie, that they've got units out everywhere searching. They keep asking the same questions, *Can they think of anywhere he might be likely to go? Any family, relatives, favourite holiday destinations?*

Eventually Kya's Mum screams, 'For God's sake, I've told you this a hundred times! They've been gone since Friday night!' It's Sunday now. They've been gone two nights.

## Kya

Time stands still. Mum is clutching Lizzie's Bunny. Her cheek is bruised, blue and purple, like a bad peach. In a few more days it will be yellowy green. He must have thumped her with all his might and the images in my mind fill me with rage. I turn my thoughts to Lizzie and my heart breaks when I think that wherever she is, whatever she's going through, she hasn't even got Bunny. She can't sleep without Bunny! The thought kills me. I can't let myself think of what he might have done to her. I pray that Mum was right all these years, that because she's his *proper daughter,* he'd never hurt her. I pray that, despite the fact he's clearly got something wrong with him, mentally, he will at least keep his hands off her.

The police officers who have been here all along sit quietly at the kitchen table, checking their phones and notebooks periodically. Zak's mum is still buzzing around. *Anyone for more tea?* No one wants anymore fucking tea! Why do people drink tea when something happens? Let's have a cup of *magic tea,* like it will fix everything. *Have a cup of tea, you'll feel better. Have a cup of tea, it'll help.* It'll help? How? Has it got magic medicine in it? Will it bring my baby sister back? The policewoman receives something on her radio and although I can't make out the muffled words, there's something about the look on her face.

'Excuse me for a moment,' she says, and leaves the room, her colleague following.

The anxiety in the room is palpable. Even Zak's mum has stopped buzzing around. The pair come back in, looking sombre.

'I'm afraid we have bad news,' the police officer says, in a soft but neutral voice that doesn't quite match the sorrow and regret on her face.

Mum is crying again, begging her, *for God's sake please tell me!* The policewoman's face looks pained and she takes a breath, tells my mum to sit down.

'They've found his car.'

Mum is screaming, '*Where, where? Where are they?*'

'I'm afraid the car has been involved in an accident. We don't know all the details, we're waiting for further information, but I'm so sorry to tell you, there were no survivors.'

I hear a deep guttural howl and it takes a moment to realise it's coming from Mum. My vision goes blurry, my knees buckle beneath me, and then I vomit on the floor.

## Zak

I have to physically hold Kya up. Mum hands me a tissue and I wipe her mouth but she pushes me away and starts screaming.

Her mum is pummeling the chest of the policeman and screaming '*No, not my baby! No!*' and he's trying to hold her arms to stop her hitting him, trying to calm her down, and I don't know what to do so I just fall to the floor with Kya and hold her as she sobs and shakes, and as I hold her, my mum holds me, and we are all crying and it's at this exact moment I know the answer to the primary philosophical question I've contemplated all these years – there is no fucking God. How can there be?

## Kya

My insides are on fire, my body still retching despite the fact there's nothing left inside. Zak is outside the toilet, won't let me out of his sight. I slump down on the toilet floor, clutch my knees to my chest and rock back and forth. *I didn't protect her, I didn't protect her, I didn't protect her.* And just when I think my eyes are empty, they well up again. But I'm angry now, full of regret and self-loathing, and I pound my fists on the plastic toilet lid until it cracks. I stand up and look in the mirror and I don't recognise the face that stares back at me. *You didn't protect her!* I scream inside my head. *You didn't protect her!* And I smack at the glass with my fists, again and again, screaming and howling, drowning out the sound of Zak shouting my name as he thumps on the door.

## Zak

Eventually she opens the bathroom door, and I notice the smashed glass from the mirror that's collected in the sink, then the blood on her hands. *Crimson regret.*

'Jesus, Kya,' I say gently as I take her hands to inspect them. Blood is running from her knuckles but she doesn't seem to register any pain, she just stares blankly ahead, repeating words so quietly they're barely audible,

'I didn't protect her, I didn't protect her, I didn't protect her.'

## Lizzie

I don't know where Daddy's gone, he said he had to go out in the car and get some things and the nice lady at the beddy breakfast said she'd watch me. She has given me the biggest bowl of ice cream ever. I couldn't decide between strawberry or chocolate so she gave me both. It's so cold it makes my brain freeze. The nice lady has gone into another room and is whispering into a phone but really loudly, and saying *I'm sure it's her! I offered to look after her. No, I don't know where he's gone,* and I know she's talking about me because she says, *She's fine, she's fine, she's eating ice cream.* I finish my ice cream and then a police lady with yellow hair comes in and tells me she's taking me home to Mummy.

## Kya

'You're squishing me!' Lizzie says, and I laugh and say *Sorry, sorry, sorry!* I can't stop kissing her and Mum won't stop crying and saying *My baby's back, she's here, she's really here!* and hugging her, and we're all hugging and laughing and sobbing, and just when I think it's physically impossible for human beings to produce any more tears, we all cry again. Lizzie is unharmed, but she keeps stroking Mum's face and asking *Why did Daddy hit you, Mummy?* and *Where is Daddy now?* Mum looks at me and my heart breaks for my baby girl. To me, he was a hateful creep, a venomous bully, but to her, he was her daddy, and now we have to tell her that her daddy is dead.

## Zak

Karma – the universal teacher that governs the balance of energy within a system of morality. When you believe in karma, as I always have, you know there is no need for revenge, you just sit back and wait, bide your time, knowing that those who do wrong will eventually get what's coming to them. As they say, if you cast a negative net you can't expect a positive catch, meaning, if you do bad things, bad things will happen to you; do good, and good things will find you. Monsters like him eventually show their true colours and will always, in this life or the next, get their comeuppance, and if karma's feeling particularly generous then it will let those that got hurt in the process sit back and watch.

## Lizzie

Mummy says Daddy is in heaven with his mummy and daddy. They hug me and tell me everything will be ok and that we are all together and we are safe and nothing will ever come between us again. Mummy keeps saying sorry to Kya and I wonder what she's done? I ask Kya if you get packed lunches in heaven and this makes her cry even more and she hugs me again. Kya and Mummy are crying and hugging a lot today, and that lady from the services is here again. Mummy says she is just here to make sure we're all ok. I ask Mummy if I can write a letter to Daddy in heaven and she says *Of course you can, my darling*, so I go to my room and get my best crayons out. Then I remember, I forgot to ask how do you get a letter to heaven? Maybe you have to buy special stamps.

## Zak

I always believed life would have a way of making things work out in the end. And it has. And I thank the universe for that. I thank the universe for my second chance at life. I thank the universe for Kya, and for what's yet to come for us, because I have a feeling it's going to be better than anything either of us ever imagined. Because guess what, *I'm always right!*

## Kya

Zak was right, things have a funny way of working out, and what doesn't kill us makes us stronger.

We're all in Mum's bed, me, Mum and Lizzie, cuddled up. I know we will be fine now. It's just us. I'm so exhausted that sleep soon pulls me down into its grip. In my dream I'm walking through the graveyard. It's dusk, and all is quiet, eerily so. My hummingbird appears, hovering in front of my face, and I sense there is urgency in its message. *What are you trying to tell me?* It flies a short way ahead, staying at eye level, stopping momentarily to look back and check I'm following, which despite the unease I feel, I am. *I thought it was all over now? What's left to warn me about?* My tiny friend leads me past the gravestones and right to the perimeter of the graveyard where it turns into woods. I've never been this far before. I stop. My hummingbird flies back to me and hovers in front of my face, its tiny black eyes looking into mine. *Follow me!* I push through some undergrowth, thistles and overgrown leaves and then I see it. His car. His big, silver estate car wrapped around a tree, the front panels crushed in. I stand stock still. *Why am I seeing this?* My hummingbird is next to me, I can hear its tiny wings flapping as it hovers just above my shoulder. It turns its head to me. *Look through the window. You need to see this to believe it's over.* I walk slowly and with trepidation, twigs snapping underneath my feet. There is no glass left in the window, just sharp jagged fragments. I look through, and strangely, what I see doesn't unnerve me at all. I know I am meant to see this. Closure. I am calm as I look at him, his head twisted round, lolling on one shoulder. His face is grey, his eyes bulging, his tongue black and hanging out of his mouth. I feel a strange sense of peace, knowing he will never have a red-faced fit again. He will never call me a freak or a disgrace or a loser again. He will never again froth at the mouth and eject spittle at me as he yells. He will never again hurt Mum, or get an opportunity to hurt Lizzie. And finally, I realise with bitter jubilation, *You won't get to hurt ME ever again!*

Now I'm in a huge, spacious room, all light and airy. I don't recognise it but it has a nice feel. A large arched window is open and a white lace curtain flaps gently in the breeze. There is nothing in the room but a round table, and on the table is a glass bell jar. My hummingbird is in the jar. I smile at it as I move towards it, then I peer closely, marvelling one last time at its feathers of iridescent turquoise, teal, violet, purple. All the pretty colours. *It's time,* I communicate without making a sound. I lift the lid of the bell jar and the hummingbird flies up to my face and hovers gently. *You're free!* I say, silently. *Fly!* And away it flies through the open window, pausing briefly to look back at me, and then it's gone. I know I won't see it again, for like this little bird, I too am finally free.

# Afterword

Many people are certain they would recognise abusive behaviour if it were happening, either to themselves or to someone close to them, and most people believe they would never allow such harmful behaviour to continue. Many people think that they would spot an abusive person a mile off, that they'd *be able to tell* if someone posed a risk to a child. The scary thing is, it's actually quite rare that a person who is harming a child, or is capable of harming a child, is one of those creepy-looking characters who look or act a certain way. The truth is, it's sometimes the people we least expect to harm a child that can and actually do violate the trust that's bestowed upon them. This is why there are so many children experiencing abuse today, and why it's often so shocking to people when a certain case comes to light. We hear people say things like '*We lived next door to him for twenty years and he always seemed so normal!*' or '*I can't believe she would do that, she was always so kind and caring!*' or '*He doesn't look like the type of person who would do such a thing!*' Of course they don't – people who pose a risk to children (or adults) don't always look a certain way, perhaps the way we imagine them to look – repellent, freak-ish, sinister, lecherous – and they certainly don't wear a sign on their forehead branding them a *paedophile* or *emotional bully*. So what does an abusive person actually look like? More often than not they are everyday folk who walk amongst us, unde-tected, charming even, and this is one of the reasons abuse can go unnoticed. The scary truth is, loving parents can hurt children, attentive and generous grandparents can hurt chil-dren, devoted teachers or adventurous and fun-loving camp leaders can hurt children. The same goes for inspirational reli-gious figures, jolly babysitters, protective brothers or sisters, cousins, the kids next door – they can all harm children. As humans we tend to put people in a box or label them as either *good* or *bad*, but we forget that seemingly good people can also have bad qualities or behaviours, behaviours that can be harmful to children. Of course, we wouldn't knowingly let our children be cared for by *bad* people, and because we think of certain people as *good*, we assume they must be wholly good, and therefore ignore or bend certain facts to fit our reassuring expectations. This is how, unfortunately, people can fail to see risk when it's staring them in the face. It then comes as a great shock to learn that a seemingly *fun uncle* or *caring teacher* or whoever, has violated their position and harmed a child.

These can be isolated events, or in other cases, like Kya's, abuse can be ongoing, and some adults may, somewhere, in the deep dark recesses of their minds, know or suspect some-thing is happening. As difficult as it may be to accept, there are many genuine, compelling reasons that it can be chal-lenging for adults, even loving parents, to take action to protect a child, or to even notice when a child is being abused, or is at risk of abuse. Such reasons may include a physical, emotional, or financial dependency on a person. In Kya's mum's case she was dependent on her husband, and she feared she would lose the seemingly safe, secure family life that he provided if she rocked the boat. He wielded all the power and control, she had no financial independence, and she couldn't imagine starting over or bringing two children up on her own. He was also a well-respected member of the community who held a prominent position, and she believed he would always *win*, and possibly even take Lizzie away from her, if anyone challenged him. It was easier for her to pretend everything was ok, or that everything would get better, and just carry on. Tragically, such thinking gets in the way of protecting children. Even intelligent, responsible people sometimes act as if it's only the evil and creepy people like the ones on the TV who hurt children.

In some cases, a child may worry or think that what's happening to them isn't really *abuse* or *isn't enough to be taken seriously*, like when Kya worried her teacher would laugh at her if she told him her stepdad was calling her names or simply making her *feel* unsafe. A child might worry that if there is no physical proof such as marks or bruises, they may not be believed, or may be told to stop exaggerating or causing trouble.

A child may be brave enough to tell an adult what's going on, seeking protection and help, like Kya did, only to be met with disbelief, denial, blame, or even punishment. What Kya legitimately experienced as a betrayal seemed to be the best her mum could do at the time, which doesn't make it ok, just tragically human and real. Please know that it is not ok to suffer the effects of mental, emotional, physical or sexual abuse, and if someone doesn't listen to you or take you seriously, someone else will – a teacher, a relative, a doctor, a friend's parent, the police, someone from a helpline, there are people out there who can help you, and who want to help you. You have the right to feel safe, to be safe, at all times, and you should not have to suffer in any way.

So please, if you or someone you know (grown-up or

child) is experiencing abuse of any kind, whether it's emotional, physical, mental or sexual abuse, please be as brave as you can and speak up.

## Links to helplines:

National Domestic Abuse Helpline
https://www.nationaldahelpline.org.uk/

Women's Aid
https://www.womensaid.org.uk/information-support/

NSPCC
https://www.nspcc.org.uk/

Childline
https://www.childline.org.uk/

If you are in an emergency situation please call 999.

## Thank you

Thank you for reading Hummingbird.

If you enjoyed the book, please do leave a review
on Amazon. Your help spreading the word about this book
would be very much appreciated. Thank you.

Love, Fran x

## About the Author

Fran Grant is an author and a book-worm. She lives in Yorkshire, United Kingdom, with her three sons. If she's not writing, she'll usually be found reading in her comfiest pyjamas, whilst eating chocolate.

Follow me on Instagram @fran_grant_writer
Follow me on Facebook @frangrantwriter
www.frangrant.com

Printed in Great Britain
by Amazon

62844435R10161